DRIVEN

What Consumes Your Mind
Controls Your Life

DRIVEN

JOCELYN COVINGTON

MILL CITY PRESS

Mill City Press, Inc.
2301 Lucien Way #415
Maitland, FL 32751
407.339.4217
www.millcitypress.net

Printed in the United States of America

Paperback ISBN-13: 978-1-6322-1017-3
Ebook ISBN-13: 978-1-6322-1018-0

Contents

Acknowledgments

To my beautiful children Nyohmee' and Kyrie, Mommy will always have your back. Remember to always follow your dreams, no matter what it takes. When someone tells you that you cannot do something, do not believe them. The sky's the limits for your dreams. To Dominique, you always have my back, and I could not ask for a better sister or right hand. To my mom and my sisters, you all stick by me, and I could not ask for a better support system or family. We have grown as a family, and I love you all.

Introduction

*H*ello ladies, I hope you are in good spirts. If not, maybe this book will put you in the right mood. My name is Jocelyn Covington. I never knew how strong I was until I had to forgive someone who was not sorry and accept an apology I never received. I am a single parent of two children. I decided to write this book to put some things into perspective.

A lot of people have doubted me and told me that I could never balance my life or that I would always struggle. Which is not correct or true? I have proved so many people wrong, and I am continuing on my journey to do so. I always had to learn to do these things for myself and not anyone else because my actions will show it. I decided to write these series of books because I wanted to give women in my shoes a voice. I love the show *Being Mary Jane* for many reasons, but what I really love is how she used to have all of those sticky notes with quotes on them on her mirror. Also, I liked when each episode. It used to be a quote before the episode started. I added quotes in my book to get you thinking about certain life events that you may have experienced.

I want the world to stop seeing us as victims. We are more like strong individuals. We as women go through all types of things on a day-to-day basis. We hide our true selves and our feelings from the world because of the way the world wants us to be. As a woman, you feel as if the world is on your shoulders because normally we do carry the weight of the world on our shoulders. We deal with life, children, social life, friendships, different relationships, responsibilities, and sacrificing. Then the way the world looks at us, we are supposed to look a certain way and act a certain way. That is not true because all women are beautiful no matter the shape, size, or color.

The things that you go through, someone else is going through, and you would be surprised who is going through what you are, believe it or not. Maybe they are even worse off than you are. Never feel as if you are alone because you are not. Always have an outlet when you are going through something—I repeat—do not hold it in. Talk to someone who will not judge you and who will understand you. We do not need those types of people in our lives. Stress kills, and you have a lot to live for these days, whether you are aware of it or not.

I put different quotes in this book because an encouraging word can take you a long way. It makes you think of different things and how you interpret the quotes your way. Sometimes we need that encouraging word. To get you through your day or something that will be on your mind. So, sit back and enjoy this book. The four different women in this book have different scenarios you can relate to, so keep an open mind. Their lives unfold right in front of you. Just think about whether you have been in the situation and see if you could handle things differently than what you have been doing. Remember a good glass of wine or two is always recommended for you to have a good read in front of you.

"The woman who does not require validation from anyone is the most feared individual on the planet."
—Mohadesa Najumi

Chapter 1

Ladies' Night

"Pour yourself a drink, put on some lipstick, and pull yourself together."
—Elizabeth Taylor

Beep, beep, beep, the streets of Boston are busy on this Friday night in a city that never sleeps, as they say. Who are they, anyway? It was a light drizzle outside. It was just enough to wet your weave, but not enough to mess up your makeup. Alex had wet and wavy hair on her head that Michelle had just installed two days before. Alex had just left her office from a long day, and she was going to meet her girls at their fave spot. Ladies, you always need a time to wind down. All work and no play cannot be good for the soul. Alex pulled up to the club and stepped out of her new-to-her 2018 Mercedes Benz C-Class C300. She had on six-inch stiletto red bottoms, as she stepped onto the wet ground. It had rained earlier that day, so she was careful because it was still drizzling a little. Alex walked around her car and clicked the lock button on her key fob. Alex then handed her keys to the guy standing in front of the club.

"Hey, Tommy, you know what to do," said Alex as she tossed him the keys to her car.

"Yes, ma'am," said Tommy.

She walked through the front door of The Underground. Alex never stood in lines when she went to events or the club. *Who does that anymore?* Alex thought to herself. Alex kept walking toward the front door. Maybe regular people did, but Alex was not regular and far from it.

Manny was at the door per usual, and he knew who Alex was. He always watched her in a stalker type of way, but Alex was not worried; that was just his personality. Alex still had a little hood in her, and she stayed strapped with her nine-millimeter named Maggie. The background behind Maggie, her gun, was simple. She was a black woman who had to protect herself and her child. Alex believed that everyone should carry. Just know that they were always together. She had been a member of the club for a minute, and it is where she got her connections from most of the time, when it came to her business.

"Hey, Miss Douglas," said Manny.

"Hey sweetheart, how are you tonight?" asked Alex as she passed him.

"I'm good now Miss Douglas," said Manny. Alex smirked at him and kept walking into the club. He watched her as she walked in and admired her ass, of course. Men will be men and are more interested in your assets than the mind you have. Alex walked through the door with metal detectors. I know what you may be thinking: how can she walk through the metal detectors with her gun. Let me break it down for you. Alex kept her gun in her purse, but her purse was always laid on the counter. It never went through the metal detectors.

Alex was well connected, and Latrice, the girl who sat in the front, was always there. Alex placed her purse on the counter,

2

and then she walked through the metal detectors. Alex always slid her a little extra money for turning a blind eye, for bringing her gun in the club.

"I got you Miss Douglas," says Latrice. Alex winked and kept walking. Alex walked through the crowds of people to get to her table where her girls were sitting. The walk through the crowded club with dancing, drinking, mingling and laughing going on was one of Boston's finest. Alexandria Douglas, yeah, that's her name, was a successful real estate agent and business owner of a private computer company. She puts the S in success and the D in

"Damn, Girl, I see you, Alex," as her friends called her over to their table. The Underground night club was where she met her girls for a celebration of the New Year coming in. It was 2019, and it was coming in so strong.

Now the Underground is the hottest night club in Boston; only the elite of elite are allowed in. If your name is not known or ringing in these streets, then you are not allowed in. You must get invited in by a member of the club. Not only does your name need to ring, but you must be doing things in these streets, not all good, but you get the picture. I am just not the one to judge you. It is not only for blacks; it is for everyone, no race or preference. The Underground is known for having professional basketball players, football players, doctors, lawyers, preachers, professors, even major drug dealers, and many others; they do not discriminate. Yes, I said drug dealers because there are some in the world that can hang with the other ballers. Some are a little smarter in what they do.

The Underground is the talk of the town; you cannot just be on a list. It is more of a membership or a partnership that is also networking with other professionals. You never know who you will meet or run into. The Underground was known for the best food and drinks. When you come to the Underground, you know that you are getting excellent service no matter what. The owner, Thompson, happened to be one of Alex's clients. She talked him into his amazing property for him and his family. Alex did not have to really sell him because the property spoke for itself. She has an eye for certain things and picked out the best properties that Boston had to offer. So, he always looked out for Alex and her friends whenever they came to the Underground.

Thompson just knew good character, and that is what Alex had. As Alexandria walked in, all eyes were on her. Heads turned to watch her walk to the table. Her hips switched from side to side as she walked in her six-inch, red-bottom stilettos. Her tight-fitted red leather dress hugged her coke-bottle-shaped body. The dark-skinned beauty had this glow on her skin that everyone saw, and you damn near needed to wear shades to look at her. Little did they know it was the coconut oil that she rubbed on her body every day, but that's our little secret, so keep your mouth closed on that tea. You must have that confidence about you no matter what other people say and always take care of self. Some might say what waist; Alex knew she was the truth, and no one could tell her different. Her hair was long down her back, thanks to her awesome hairstylist Michelle who was one of her best friends. When she walked, her hair bounced off the top of her tight-round ass. "Love yourself first, and everything else falls into line. You really have to love yourself to get anything done in this world" was what Lucille Ball said.

It's lady's night tonight, and the girls are celebrating different accomplishments for their success to end the year. This is something that the girls had been doing every year for the last couple of years and counting. Alex calls Camilla to see where she is. Camila puts the L in late as hell; the girl would be late to her own darn funeral if she was not already dead. Camilla had no sense of urgency in her blood whatsoever. Camilla thought she was royalty, but that's her parents' fault—they treated her like that. She was that friend you had to trick and tell her the wrong time for her to show up at the right time. The rest of the girls were there, and she was the only one missing as always. Camilla Washington is one of Alex's best friends since the sandbox.

"Girl, where are you?" says Alex.

"Hello, I can't hear you, but I am on my way, I had to close the office and finish up this business deal for the year.

"Where is Honestie and Michelle?" asked Camilla.

Alex yells into the phone, "I'm looking at them now. They are here already, and we are waiting on your ass to get here." Alex hung up the phone because the music was too loud. The music is jumping in the Underground, and the men are out tonight, looking to mingle. It was the best night to celebrate and get out on the town to have a little bit of fun. Hell, even come into the new year with a little tender or two. The night is young, and the girls ready to get into somethings, well at least some of them not all.

Alex walks through the crowd to get to the table with her girls. The girls had a reserved table every time they came to the club. The section kind of had their names on it. Honestie, and Michelle got up to greet Alex and compliment her on her outfit.

"You look great, boo" says Alex, to Honestie.

"Thank you, hun," says Honestie.

"Work it, girl," says Alex to Michelle.

"Yes, I know I'm bad," says Michelle as she laughs. They all hugged and sat down at the round red table. Cocktails were already on the table from the other two ladies.

"I see the party has started without me; neither one of you all could wait, I see," says Alex. Honestie is bobbing her head and scoping out the scene to look at the eye candy as she calls it.

"We were thirsty, hun. What you want us to do, swallow our spit all night?" asked Michelle.

Alex hung around women who were doing something with their lives. You need to always have people in your corner to motivate you. The world has enough outside haters. Have people in your corner, who make your life easier and cheer you on. Alex had three best friends. There was Honestie Robinson who Alex met at a networking that Alex went years ago. Alex and Honestie got to talking, and afterward, Alex sold Honestie her second home. They have been friends ever since.

Honestie is the CEO of the company her late father, Mr. Gerald Hide. They made all-natural products for black women and men, which were anything that you could think of for skin care, hair care, and essential oils. They were contracted with a bunch of different stores around the world. Her father left her the company when he passed away from a brain tumor, which was unexpected. This chick knows how to make a dollar into a million dollars literally; that's why her father trusted her with his company and not her siblings. Honestie is engaged to a handsome man named Paul Mathis who would give her the world if she asked for it. She could not wait to be Mrs. Mathis.

Then there is Michelle Lewis, a professional hairstylist. Alex and Michelle met through their daughters' gymnastics team. They started to do play dates and clicked from there. Michelle does all the celebrity's hair when they come into town in addition to the ones who live in town. Michelle does all the girls' hair in the group; it is more like a girl code, you know. You must have a friend who does hair when you are in certain professions. It's a hook up, but not really because you are still paying full price. You support your friend. She still sometimes gives the girls a discount. She has made her living off her hair-care products, and the way they smelled made you think God came down and touched your scalp.

This made your hair healthy and fabulous, which is how she made her coins. I just want to spit a little knowledge on Alex's homegirls really quickly because they were bomb.

"How are things looking tonight, ladies?" says Alex.

Honestie replies, "I see some snacks in here tonight." (A snack means someone who is good looking or someone who looks like something.)

"Potential husbands in the future I see," as she laughs.

"I'm just playing; y'all know I have Paul's fine ass. I can look at the appetizers on the menu, but I cannot taste a thing, not even a damn appetizer," says Honestie. Alex and Michelle look at Honestie and burst out laughing.

"You need help," says Alex.

"Has anyone talked to Camilla?" asked Honestie.

Michelle rolls her eyes and looks over at Alex, saying, "Where is your bestie?"

Then there was Camilla Washington. She and Alex grew up together. She was a broker at her company, and she could sell any building you put in front of her. She was in charge of selling apartment buildings, warehouses, and storefronts. This is how she made her money. Camilla really did not have to work because her parents had money. Camilla did not want to live off of her parents because they had too many rules, so she made her own way.

I can imagine what you are thinking—here goes the drama, right? Now the reason for the shade and the conflict between Camilla and Michelle is simple and petty as hell, but you know how women can be. Though each woman has her own money, it is always something with these two women. The best-friend code is to support each other by any means necessary, no matter what. Here is the current problem of the two if you were wondering. If you were not, I'm going to tell you anyway so sit back and listen to this tea, hun.

Camilla had a presentation with some very important investors that could not be rescheduled because they were international clients. She would lose her bonus and the client, so changing that meeting was not an option. She needed to get her hair done badly, and as you can see, Camilla is a big procrastinator and always late as hell. She waited too late to schedule her appointment, and this time just so happened to be play-off weekend. So, Michelle was booked with all the Boston Celtics' wives and any celebrities who were in town. All the girls knew that play-off weekend was off limits because that is when Michelle makes the most money. The girls never booked their appointments this particular weekend or if they did, they knew to book their appointments accordingly. All the girls knew this upfront, so there was no confusion.

When Camilla walked into Michelle's shop an hour and a half late to her appointment, Michelle was booked up and had no way to even squeeze her in. So, Camilla took it upon herself and left Michelle's shop. She then went to Michelle's competition, knowing that the outcome would be bad, but she did not care. All she thought about was her and her hair. Camilla called it a judgment call, and Michelle is still salty about it. Camilla calls everything a judgment call when she knows that she is wrong.

Alex flips her hair and looks at Michelle.

"Damn girl, you still mad about that hair situation, or is there something else this time?" asked Alex.

Michelle sucks her teeth and says to Alex, "Now if that heifer went to another real estate agent, then you would be salty as well. Now wouldn't you?" says Michelle. Before Alex could part her lips to say anything or answer Michelle, Camilla then walks up to greet the ladies and sat down. Camilla sits next to Honestie, as the waitress walks over to take more drink orders.

"I guess the second round is on me, since I am late as always," says Camilla.

Alex asked the waitress for menus, and she pulled some menus out of her belt and handed Alex the menus. As Alex looks over the menu, she looks up, and her eye is caught by a tall, dark, and handsome man from across the room.

"Damn," says Alex, under her breath as she tries to look away. The man was across the room. He is standing six feet, four inches and weighs 250 pounds or so, with hazel eyes and nothing but muscle. He was wearing a nice, slick, pressed blue Armani suit, a fresh hair cut with deep ocean waves, a gold pinky ring on each finger, and Armani shoes on his feet. His arms are solid as a rock as if he goes to the gym or something; you can tell he takes care of his body because of how he was cut up. Alex could tell a man's body structure from a mile away. I told you she had an eye for this stuff. The nice Rolex sits on his wrist, and he had legs of a God, as though Zeus was his daddy or something.

Yes, she could see all that from where she was sitting. All she could say was *Yassssss* in her head. Alex then sits up in her chair with her back straight up, and her legs crossed slightly. Any woman knows that when a woman is getting noticed, she must keep it cute, always with just a little bit of etiquette. When he smiled, all thirty-two pearly white teeth sparkled in his mouth. His skin was glowing, and his lips were plumped. Alex swore that the heavens gates opened, and a halo was around this man's head. Some may say that she is doing too much or overreacting, but you had to see what she saw through her eyes. This man had to be the one, but she was not going to jump ahead of herself.

Alex not knowing that the waitress had returned to the table, ready to take their orders.

Michelle breaks Alex's focus, "Damn, girl, are you going to order? We are waiting on you," says Michelle.

"Sorry, you all, I got distracted," says Alex.

Camilla looks at Alex and says, "I see why she is distracted. Hell, I would be too—look at him," says Camilla. Camilla was always in the mix and never missed a beat, with her nosey ass.

Alex looks at Camilla and says, "Shut up," as she orders her food. All the girls place their orders, and it was the same as usual for everyone.

"The DJ is on it tonight, isn't he? He is not playing with us tonight. I'm about to get out of this seat and shake this ass," says Michelle.

"Me too, girl; I came to turn up," says Honestie. The waitress walks back over to the table, interrupting the girls as they are talking; she has a drink in her hand.

"Excuse me, ma'am, this is from the fine brother in the blue suit over there by the bar," says the waitress. Alex looks up, raises the glass, and nods her head at the man. She placed the drink on the table. Camilla is the loud and outspoken friend; like I said she is nosey as hell. She is always the one to speak up out in the group before anyone else could.

"Girl, a nod, what is your problem? That's it? You better walk over there, or I will," says Camilla. Alex looks over at Camilla and rolls her eyes.

"I bet you will," says Alex. As Alex is about to talk, all the ladies start to repeat her.

"It's a new year, and I do not have time for the bullshit from these men. I must focus on me and my goals. I have my daughter who needs me. I am too successful and have come too far to give these cookies up to anything that may look good or smell good. At this point in my life I'm not getting younger, I want something real."

"Blah, blah, blah, girl. Are you done yet?" says all the girls in unison. "Here you go with this hopeless romantic shit. You need that cookie bitten into, like the cookie monster. It's been a while—it is cobwebs down there," says Michelle. "All the girls laugh and look at Alex.

"Ya'll are not going to come for me tonight; y'all can all kick rocks," says Alex.

"Speaking of cookies, Camilla, how was your date with Jacob?" asked Michelle. Jacob was just an appetizer on Camilla's menu of many men.

"I'm so sick of these men; none of them can get right," says Camilla.

Honestie laughs at Camilla. "He won't be around for long, so the cookie stays up until further notice," says Camilla. Now Camilla changes men like she changes her drawers but not on purpose; she has a commitment issue that she cannot seem to shake. Camilla does not have sex with these men because she values her body and morals, mind you, she picks on Alex for the same morals.

"Where is this waitress with our food? Her tip is counting on it," says Honestie.

"I had to work through lunch; I'm hungry," says Michelle.

"The chick just took our order ten minutes ago, ma'am; calm down," says Camilla. As the girls laugh, the waitress returns to the table with a rose and their food. As the waitress is about to walk off, she is stopped by Alex.

"Who is the rose for?" says Alex.

The waitress turns around and says, "You—the gentleman who sent the drink sent the rose as well." Everyone turns to Alex to wait for a response. Alex never cracked under pressure. You never could see her sweat.

"Someone is trying to get someone's attention," says Camilla. Alex looks down, she shakes her head and smiles.

"Can I eat in peace, please? He can wait," says Alex. Alex thought to herself, *What does this man want from me?*

The girls eat, drink, and laugh to success and all their accomplishments made in the year. After eating, the girls decide to go to the dance floor. The girls head to the dance floor to dance before the night is over. The DJ was not letting up, and he was playing songs that made you want to twerk. Walking to the dance floor, Alex's hand is grabbed, and she turns to look who has her hand. She is stopped by the man in the suit. Alex starts to sweat a little because this man is to fine.

When she looks at him, their eyes meet, and it is an instant connection. The chemistry was there, there was no doubt about that. Alex could feel her vagina about to jump out her dress. The rest of the girls continue to walk to the floor and leave Alex talking to the gentlemen.

"May I have my hand back?" asked Alex.

"Yes, you can if you talk to me gorgeous lady. My name is Jamal Stevenson and yours?" asked Jamal.

"Alexandria Douglas, but my real friends call me Alex. Nice to meet you," says Alex. Alex did not even want to play hard ball or hard to get with him because he was so fine.

"I have been trying to get your attention all night, sweetheart. Why are you avoiding me?" says Jamal.

"I'm not avoiding you; I'm just enjoying my night," says Alex.

"Then what do you call it, Ms. Dark Chocolate?" asks Jamal.

"I am here with my girls, celebrating, so I'm focused on nothing else," says Alex. Camilla and Honestie yell for Alex and signals her to come on, as they are shaking their ass on the dance floor. Her friends knew how to party. Alex nods her head at the girls and signals them to chill.

"I see you are wanted, but I want to finish the conversation" says Jamal. As he stares into her hazel eyes again. Jamal is intrigued by what he sees in Alex.

"They will be okay," says Alex. Jamal laughs.

"You said you are celebrating. What might that be, if you do not mind me asking," says Jamal.

"Well since you are being nosey, Mr. Stevenson," says Alex. Alex looks at him and says "Success."

"You are the most gorgeous person I have ever seen; I want to get to know more about you," says Jamal. Alex hesitates because of everything she stands for and been through; she is thinking if she should go back through this again.

"Why do you want to get to know me?" asks Alex.

"I like what I see, and it looks mighty good," says Jamal.

"Thank you for that," says Alex as she sits down on the stool next to Jamal. "I am something to look at, though," says Alex. She was very confident in herself.

"Confidence—I like it," says Jamal.

"Why are you here tonight?" asked Alex.

"I wanted to get out the house. I was supposed to meet my friend, but he bailed on me," says Jamal.

"That is too bad," says Alex.

"What do you do for a living?" asks Jamal.

"You get straight to the point," says Alex.

"I have to because I do not want your time or mine wasted, sweetheart," says Jamal. *A man who gets it*, Alex thought to herself.

"I agree with that fully. I am a real estate agent, and I am an investor in a computer company," says Alex. "And you?"

"Okay, beauty and brains, but I am a defense attorney for Johnson & Simpson Law Firm," says Jamal. Little did Alex know Jamal was a major defense lawyer at a prestigious law firm in Boston, and he was not just a regular man.

"So, you help the bad guys?" says Alex.

"Something like that," says Jamal as he smiles. Alex turns to look at the dance floor where her friends were having fun.

"Would you like a drink?" asks Jamal.

"No, thank you, I have had one too many, and I have to be to work tomorrow," says Alex.

"Work?" says Jamal.

"Yes, I have to work," says Alex.

"Okay, can I get your number? I will let you get back to your friends," says Jamal. Alex looks at Jamal and goes into her Chanel bag to pull out her business card.

"Here, you can use it if you want," says Alex.

"Trust me; I will use it," says Jamal.

"Well, if it is okay with you, I am going to get back to my friends," says Alex. "Nice to meet you."

"No, it was my pleasure" says Jamal, as he bites his bottom lip. You could tell he moisturized his lips because of how soft they looked.

Alex gets up to walk away. Her hair bounces off her ass as she walks to the dance floor to meet the girls. She did not look back, once she walked off. The way you walk can tell a person a lot about you. An unspoken girl's rule clearly states that you never let a man see your desperation or see you sweat. This man must never know how you feel about them out the gate. Once you walk away, you do not look back—ever. Keep walking; you have to keep him guessing that way. If he is really that into you, he is watching you walk away, and he will definitely call. Alex's hips twist from side to side, and as you guessed, Jamal watched her walk away. I told you that he would.

The ladies danced all night while drinking and laughing. Jamal watched her and her friends, while admiring Alex from a distance, but not in a creepy type of way. Jamal just wanted to know her better; he had to know who this chick was. He could not figure out what it was about her. He never wanted anyone so badly. It was more than sex with him. Alex looked up to see if Jamal was still at the bar. Jamal nodded at Alex, and she smiled. All the girls looked at Alex in suspense.

"What happened over there? he has not moved," asks Michelle.

"Nothing yet," says Alex as she bites her bottom lip.

"Oh, no, ma'am" says Camilla.

"What?" says Alex.

"You have not been like this in a while," says Honestie. Alex just looked that the girls. She did not want to tell them how she really felt. She for sure had butterflies. This was the first time she felt this in a while, and she craved for more of it.

"We will have a conference call tomorrow," says Alex.

"A conference call?" asks Camilla.

"Yes, a conference call," says Alex. Alex wanted to tell the girls everything, but it was too loud in the club, and she did not want to seem too excited.

Alex was ready for a change but did not know until that very moment what that change was going to be. When you meet someone, you always want to know what that person's intentions are. Have you ever met someone who was so mysterious that you knew they were hiding something? It is crazy dating nowadays because people don't date anymore; it is just all about sex. The ladies danced one last time. They hugged and went their separate ways.

Remember it is always okay to let your hair down sometimes. Get friends that you can have a great time with—no drama, no pressure, no bullshit, just nice clean fun.

Chapter 2

Alexandria Douglas

"People will forget what you said, people will forget what you did, but people will never forget how you made them feel."
—*Maya Angelou*

"Priscilla, do I have any messages?" asks Alex.
"Yes, you do Mrs. Douglas," says Priscilla. As Alex walks into her office, she opens her office door to sit in her chair.

Alex yells to Priscilla. "Can you come in here so that we can go over my calendar for today?" says Alex. Now if you were not paying attention in the beginning, sit back and sip this tea. Alexandria Douglas's name speaks for itself as I said before. She is one of few blacks, or African Americans if you will, in her office. In a short period of time, she made a name for herself, which did not take long. Yes, she is a woman and damn good at her job. Alex is the go-to person for all the high-end properties in Boston. Alex was also a business owner of a company she invested in when she was a little younger, a couple of years ago. It ended up making her lots of money. The company was dealing with social media and how to market your business.

At her age, she was set for life and had no worries, but she kept that a secret. You never let the right hand know what the left hand is doing; one of her mentors told her that. Priscilla was Alex's assistant, and although she was not the brightest crayon in the box, Alex dealt with her because Priscilla had potential, and Alex knew all she needed was guidance. Alex needed an assistant right away, so she called in a favor from a friend.

"You have messages from a Jamal Stevenson, you have a meeting in the conference room with the Freeman's to finish closing on their home in fifteen minutes, and after that you are free for today," says Priscilla. "The Freemans are on their way up now, and Mr. Grossman is looking for you."

"Okay, Priscilla, let Mr. Grossman know I am on the way," says Alex.

"Yes, ma'am," says Priscilla. Alexandria looks up from her glasses.

"Let me see those messages," says Alex.

Priscilla hands the messages to Alexandria and then walks out to do what Alex told her to do. Alex looks through the messages. Jamal had already called twice. Alex thinks in her mind, *Damn, he really wants me; he called already.* Alex leaves the messages on the desk and heads to the conference room to meet the Freemans and Mr. Grossman.

"Hello Freemans, this is an exciting day for you today," says Alex. "Mr. and Mrs. Freeman, this is my boss Mr. Grossman."

"We are the Freemans, how are you, sir?" they both say in unison.

"Here are the keys to your new home, and Priscilla will finish up the paperwork," says Alex. "Make sure all the highlighted parts are signed. I will be right back. I have to get something out of my office." Alex left out of the conference room and headed to her office. Her tradition was to get her clients something special because they could have gone with anyone, but they chose her.

Alex grabs a Saks Fifth basket full of goodies. She looks at her desk to look at the messages Jamal left. Alex leaves her office to go back to the conference room with the basket.

"Oh wow, you did not have to do that," says Mrs. Freeman.

"Yes, I did," says Alex.

"No, thank you, you were amazing Miss Douglas," said the Freemans.

"Not a problem," Alex says. She looks over to Priscilla to make sure that all of the documents were signed. Priscilla nodded at Alex. Alex gets up to shake their hands.

"If you need anything or you have family or friends who need me, you have my number," says Alex.

"Again, thank you, Miss Douglas," says the Freemans.

Alex walks her clients to the elevator and heads back to her office. Once she gets in her office, she sits down and stares at the messages. There were three messages, and two were from Jamal. Alex is not sure what she should do because she has not been on the dating scene for a while, and she had her reasons. Alex has been burned so many times by men, and she was tired of the bullshit. Not burned, as in STD—get your mind away from that—I had to clarify that for some of you. Just hurt, she was tired of the dead-end relationships, lies, and broken promises. All she could do was look at the messages and ruminate, until there was a knock at her office door. "Yes," says Alex.

It was her boss, Mr. Grossman. He opens the door and walked in. He always saw great potential in Alex from the first time he met her. He wanted to give her a chance to make it in this industry. She never failed him and met his needs every time it came to a property.

"Hi sir, how are you this morning?" asks Alex.

"I'm great; thanks for asking," says Mr. Grossman.

"How can I help you on this great Wednesday?" says Alex.

"I just want to let you know I am proud of you for closing that deal. That house has been on the market for months, and no one has been able to even get someone to view it. That commission is going to be something mean, and you deserve it," says Mr. Grossman.

"Mr. Grossman, that is nice of you to say, and that house had potential. It just needed the right marketing approach and a little TLC," says Alex.

Mr. Grossman laughs. "I had to talk the previous owner into some things, but it worked," says Alex. As the two were conversing, Priscilla knocked on the door.

"Yes?" says Alex.

"You might want to see this," says Priscilla.

"Are you Alexandra Douglas," asked the flower man?

"Yes, I am," says Alex. The delivery man handed the flowers to Alex.

Before Alex could say thank you to the delivery man, he said, "Come on in, boys." Alex looked puzzled. Twelve dozen roses in seven beautiful vases came in.

"Those are nice; he is a lucky guy," says Mr. Grossman as he leaves the room.

Alex laughs, "How do you know it is from a guy?" says Alex.

He pops back in to grin. "Meeting at 12:30 p.m. Look at you, Alex; it is from a guy," says Mr. Grossman.

"That is in ten minutes. I'm coming now," says Alex. Mr. Grossman nods at Alex and leaves the room.

Alex gets out of her seat to smell the flowers and read the card. It said, "To the dark-skinned beauty, I will not give up, from Jamal." Alex calls Priscilla from the other room.

"Priscilla, get Camilla on the line asap, please. Let me know once Camilla is on the line patched into my office," says Alex. The line in Alex office blinks. Alex picks up the phone.

"Hey, chick, what is up?" asks Camilla. Alex hears Camilla's music in the background, so she knew she was in the car.

"Girl, I do not know what to do about this Jamal character from the night before last. I need advice. He has left me two messages already and sent flowers to my office girl," says Alex.

"Girl, you better, you better," as Camilla laughs out loud.

"Look, focus and pay attention; I need your advice," says Alex. Camilla did not take this situation serious as she thought it was funny. She knew Alex was overreacting.

"Alex, you need some penis; you are backed up at this point," says Camilla.

"Camilla, I'm being serious right now, and I am a little backed," says Alex with an attitude. Alex and Camilla have been friend's way longer than the other girls, so their bond was thicker. They grew up together and watched each other make it from different situations. Camilla's parents had money, but they made her work for every dime, and they were extremely strict.

"Girl, call him and see what he wants. That is the only way you are going to know what big daddy wants," says Camilla as she laughs.

"Why are you calling him big daddy? Man, you need help," says Alex as she laughs.

"He looks like he is daddy material," says Camilla.

"You are so aggravating," says Alex.

"Well, chick, I have to bounce. I have this investor meeting to get to in five minutes. Call him and tell me the details later. Love you," says Camilla as she hangs up the phone. Alex was curious to see Jamal wanted with her. Alex looked at the time and headed to the meeting.

Alex walked into the conference room. "How are we doing today, team? Let's get started with some things we have going on while we wait on Mr. Grossman to come in. I have been filling in for Tom while he is out on vacation. You all have been killing it" says Alex.

"Thanks Miss Douglas," one of the agents said. Before Alex could respond to the agent, Mr. Grossman walked into the conference room and cuts Alex off.

"Sorry, Alex, but I have an announcement to make," says Mr. Grossman. Alex goes to sit down while he talks.

"Tom has decided to retire all of sudden, so the higher-ups have decided to put someone into place immediately," says Mr. Grossman. Everyone looked around the room.

"The reason for the meeting is for me to announce who that will be," says Mr. Grossman. Alex is thinking in her head so many thoughts, such as *I could be up for the position and that would be another notch in my belt.*

"We have decided to promote Alexandria Douglas to Executive Chief of Operations" says Mr. Grossman. Everyone clapped as Alex stood up. She stood around a table surrounded by only people of a different color than her, and she was pleased.

All Alex could do was say, "Thank you, God.

"Alexandria you are moving up to the sixteenth floor," says Mr. Grossman.

"I cannot thank you enough for this opportunity, sir. This means so much to me and my family" says Alex.

"This meeting is adjourned—back to work" says Mr. Grossman. Everyone walked out and congratulated Alex.

"You deserve it, your stats are the highest in the company, and with the last house you closed today, it put you over the top at 2.5 million dollars for the month," says Mr. Grossman.

"I am just doing my job," says Alex.

"You are doing more than that, but we will meet later this week with the details," says Mr. Grossman.

"I will be ready, sir," says Alex. Alex walks out of the conference room and walks back up to her now-old office to think about what happened.

Alex sat back in her chair to think about how far she has come in her life. Alex was a single mother of a beautiful little girl who she is raising by herself, and she has loved every minute of it. Alex always dreamed of having more children, but it had to be the right way. The drive that Alex had wasn't because of her getting these coins, but it was because of her daughter Leah Beloved, which was her name. Alex was determined to show Leah Beloved that no matter your circumstances, you can still win. Here is the back story with Alex's past.

Alex and Leah Beloved's father Coby Brooks were an item back in the day; they were inseparable. When you saw him, you saw her! Alex was still in college for marketing management and was a straight A student across the board. She was on a full scholarship for school. When she met Coby Brooks, she thought he was the best thing since sliced bread. The two met at a homecoming party that the college had. Coby did not go to the school, but his cousin attended the college. He was always up at the school or in the mix because he had clients there, if you know what I mean. The two instantly hit it off. Coby took her to Waffle House after the homecoming game, and they talked all night, mostly about their goals to dreams, and to even their childhoods. They had so much in common that Alex needed to know more about him. Coby grew up poor, his mom was on drugs, and his father left to marry another woman. He had to take care of and raise himself because his mother was in the streets. Coby had a lot of anger built up, and he knew it. Alex made Coby feel whole again. It got to the point where they were together every day. Alex would finish class and meet Coby at his spot. Coby taught Alex how to hustle, but the smart way. He never let her put her hands-on drugs or product. Coby wanted Alex to stay in school; he knew she was special.

They dated for a year before Alex found out she was pregnant with Leah Beloved. When she told Coby she was pregnant, he changed. He was not the man she first met or fell in love with. Coby disappeared on her. He changed his number and moved. Alex did not give up; this only pushed her to continue to keep striving for nothing but the best. People told her to get rid of Leah Beloved, or she would not make it or survive. When she was pregnant with Leah Beloved, she almost lost her, due to complications. She saw something in her daughter, and she knew that she could not get rid of her, so she kept her.

Leah Beloved's name came from Alex's grandma who was someone she could always talk to. When Alex went off to college, her grandmother gave her a necklace that had a genie lamp on it. She told Alex that she could have any wish come true if she wore it all the time and never took it off. Alex was devasted when her grandmother died of a brain tumor. She went in for a routine check-up, and it happened all of a sudden. Alex knew deep down in her heart that she was going to be raising her daughter alone because Coby was in the streets heavy, and he ghosted her.

Alex learned the hustle game from Coby, and that is the only thing he taught her, which she uses in her everyday life now. Alex used to love the bad boys and the ones who seemed tough. Alex had no respect for Coby. When he finally decided to come back around, Leah Beloved was three years old. Alex had graduated college and was entering into her career. Alex rarely let Coby see Leah Beloved. Coby always came in and out of their lives. Alex felt like a child needed structure in their lives and not being stable was not an option. Alex kept Leah Beloved busy and made sure that she was happy. Alex rarely dealt with Coby or his foolishness. Coby had a long rap sheet, and he was always in and out of jail.

Alex's focus was broken when her phone rang. Speak of the devil, here is Coby's ass calling now. Hold on one minute, pause for a cause; Alex must take this fool's call.

"Hello, how can I help you?" says Alex.

"Man, stop playing with me, Alex," says Coby.

"Coby, I cannot do this right now because I have a meeting in five minutes. What do you want?" asks Alex. She did not have a meeting; she just wanted to get him off the phone.

"Alex, you know what I want. when can I see my daughter?" says Coby.

"Coby, I do not want *my* daughter around you and the bullshit you have going on, period," says Alex.

"I have to give her birthday gift to her," says Coby.

"You got to be fucking kidding me right now; her birthday was three weeks ago, Coby," says Alex.

"I got caught up with some stuff, but I'm back in town now, and I want to make things right with her. That's my right," says Coby.

"You do not have rights. Look I have to go; I will talk to you about this later," says Alex.

"I do have the right to explain to my daughter what happened," says Coby.

"Coby, I have a business lunch to get to," says Alex.

"Alex, do not make me come find you," says Coby. Alex laughed because she knew Coby was lying.

"Bye, Coby," says Alex. Alex hangs up the phone. She did not want to talk to Coby; it was always bad energy.

Alex loved Coby, but he left her high and dry. Years later, Alex found out he left her for a chick he had met at another college. Coby did not check on Alex through her pregnancy or when Leah Beloved was born. Alex's mother told her that she would help, but her mother was a free spirit. Her mom did her own thing, and Alex did not want her mom to stop her life for her. Alex was the youngest child of two other girls.

Her sisters had already started their lives, and Alex felt behind. She never wanted sympathy from anyone. So, she hustled with her school work and her job. She got a job in the dean's office to take care of her and Leah Beloved. The secretary in the dean's office had a soft spot for Alex. She still stayed in school, even with her child. She found an apartment near campus because she could not live in the dorms with a baby. Alex graduated with Leah Beloved on her hip; it was the happiest day of her life. Alex got the opportunity to intern at the same place she works at now; she didn't sleep her way to the top like some people did. No one in the office even tried to treat her like that; they had too much respect for her.

Even though Mr. Grossman wanted her, his old ass would never tap this ass in Alex's direction. He always showed respect. Alex thought about how things would affect her daughter, so she prided herself on being a good role model for Leah Beloved. Alex is not perfect by a long shot, but she does her best by her daughter. Leah Beloved is ten years old, and she adores her mom. She looks up to her mom in so many ways and understands her mom's hustle.

Alex gets a text from Coby. LET ME SEE MY DAUGHTER, ALEX. DAMN, YOU KNOW I WILL FIND YOU. Alex looked at the text, and exited it. Alex was not trying to keep Leah Beloved away from her father, but she was protecting her baby from all his mess and the street life. Coby made a lot of promises that he never followed through with. Alex had no feelings for Coby; that ship had sailed a long time ago. She was the one that had to pick up the pieces and explain to her daughter that it was not her fault that her father was the way he was. Alex thinks to herself, *Coby can wait.* She was not bitter; she was watching out for her child. Let's make that very clear.

Alex picks up the phone, and dials Jamal's number.

"Hello, this is Jamal Stevenson," says Jamal.

Alex hesitated before she spoke. "Hello, how are you?"

"This has to be chocolate drop. I thought you would never call me, I was about to send a dove and letter next," says Jamal as he laughed.

"Do not act like you have been sitting by your phone waiting on me to call," says Alex.

"I was actually, but how are you today?" asks Jamal.

"I'm good, thanks for asking. Today is a long day already but all great news," says Alex.

"That is good, would you like to share the news?

"I got a big promotion today," says Alex.

"Promotion, okay, let's celebrate. Have you eaten today beautiful?" asks Jamal.

"No, I have not, sir, and I really do not have time to eat," says Alex.

"I know you have time; you have to eat. Everyone has to eat," says Jamal.

"Wait, wait; how do you know that I have time?" says Alex.

"Look, let me take you to a quick lunch, and I will let you get back to work. With all this talking we could have been there by now or me on the way to you," says Jamal. *I do need to eat,* she thought to herself.

"I'll be downstairs at my office in ten minutes. I will text you the address," says Alex.

"I'm around the corner, sweetie. I will be there in a minute. I don't need the address," says Jamal.

"Okay, excuse me. I will be down there in a minute," says Alex.

"It will be a black town car," says Jamal. Alex gets up to look out the window to see the black town car pulling around the corner.

"Wow, okay, I'm coming," says Alex. Alex texted all the girls in the group chat to let them know where she was going. You must always send your whereabouts to your homegirls to tell them what's going on, just in case you go missing, so the cops know who did it.

Alex grabbed both phones, her Gucci bag, and her iPad and headed out her office.

As she passes Priscilla, she says, "Route all my calls to my cell phone, I'm going to lunch."

"Yes, ma'am Miss Douglas" says Priscilla. Alex gets to the elevator, when her phone rings. It was Coby again. Alex forwarded him to voicemail and steps off the elevator in her Gucci six-inch heels. All eyes in the lobby are on her with her long twenty-eight-inch straight hair swaying from side to side. She sees a tall black man in a black suit, standing outside of a black town car.

"Ma'am, let me get that door for you," says the driver. Alex stepped in the town car and greeted Jamal.

"Hello, Miss Douglas, how are you today?" asked Jamal.

"You left me no choice" says Alex.

"I hope you are hungry; there is a place I want to take you," says Jamal.

"Well, I can eat, so where are we going?" says Alex Jamal had to control himself when he saw Alex because she looked so good.

"It is a bistro that I want to take you to right around the corner," says Jamal.

"You are going to take me to a spot you take all your chicks to?" says Alex.

"Umm, no ma'am, what type of man you take me for?" says Jamal. Alex parted her lips to answer when they pulled up to the restaurant.

"You really do not want me to answer that," says Alex. Alex gets out the car, and Jamal admires her frame. Jamal wanted to explore Alex's insides; he yearned to know more about her. They walked into the restaurant, and Jamal is greeted by the staff. An old lady came from behind the counter and hugged Jamal so tight.

"How are you, Nana?" says Jamal.

"I'm good suga, and I would ask you how you are, but I can see how you are," says Jamal's nana. Jamal laughed and introduced Alex to his nana.

"Nana, this is Miss Alexandria Douglas," says Jamal.

"Hello, ma'am, nice to meet you," says Alex.

"You as well, suga" says Jamal's nana.

"Nana, this is the woman I was telling you about," says Jamal. Alex is thinking in her head, *What does he mean?*

"Oh, this is the real estate agent, now you all look at the menu and let me know what you want," says Nana. As Alex is looking at the menu, her phone rings. Alex walks to the side to take the call.

To her non-surprise, it was Coby on the line again. "Hello, what do you want? I am at lunch, Coby," says Alex.

"I'm at your office, and we need to talk now," says Coby.

"I do not answer to you, and you can wait" says Alex. "You can make time to eat, but you cannot meet me," says Coby.

"Bye, I will talk to you later," says Alex.

Alex hangs up the phone and walks back over to order her food. Jamal stood, looking at Alex with a mysterious look on his face. This man was the sexiest thing she had ever seen. He made her nerves jump every time she looked into his eyes.

"I would like the baked chicken, yams, mac & cheese, and cabbage," says Alex. Jamal looks over at Alex and smiles. Jamal orders his food after her. They both sit down to eat as Jamal looks into Alex's eyes.

"I told my grandma about you because she has a property that is worth five hundred thousand dollars, but she is getting the run around about the property," says Jamal. Alex looks up from her plate.

"You set me up. You brought me to meet your grandmother's spot; that's not fair," says Alex.

"Well I know you wanted good food to make your day better, so I brought you here," says Jamal.

"Thank you for the business, and I will look out for your nana" says Alex.

"Congrats on your promotion as well, so it is beauty and brains, I like that," says Jamal.

"Yes, it's something like that, also you can give your grandma my number," says Alex.

"How does it taste in your mouth?" says Jamal.

Alex looked at Jamal, and she gave him that look like do not try me.

"You know what I mean, get your mind out the gutter," says Jamal.

"The food tastes great, and I will be coming back," says Alex. As they both finished up their food, Jamal got up from the table to hug his grandmother goodbye. Jamal kissed his grandmother on the forehead and headed for the door where Alex was already standing. Jamal's grandma waves to Alex, and she waves back. They both step out of the door of the restaurant to get to the car. The driver pulled the car around, and they both got in.

"So when will I see you again, Miss Douglas?" says Jamal.

"I have to check my schedule," says Alex.

"Squeeze me in somewhere; you have to eat again," says Jamal. Alex got back to the office, and Coby was standing out front.

"Shit," says Alex.

"What is wrong, baby?" says Jamal.

"Nothing I cannot handle. Thanks for lunch. I will call you later," says Alex.

"Are you sure?" says Jamal.

"I am sure," says Alex. Jamal grabs Alex's hand, and Alex turns her head before getting out the car.

"Call me," says Jamal. Alex smiles and get out of the town car. Alex grabs her belongings, shuts the door, and walks up to her building.

As Coby stopped Alex at the door, he asked, "Who the fuck is that, Alexandria?"

"I'm not sure who you are talking to or why you are even at my office, Coby," says Alex. Coby always felt like he could control Alex, because he had that "I am that nigga" mentality.

"How can I help you because you have lost your damn mind? This is my office; this is my job," says Alex.

"I told you we needed to talk," says Coby, and he raises his fingers to point in Alex's face. Before Alex could talk or say anything, they were interrupted by Jamal. He pulls up and rolls down the window.

"Is everything okay, Miss Douglas?" says Jamal.

"Bruh this has nothing to do with you, so I advise you to bounce." says Coby.

"I was talking to Miss Douglas," says Jamal.

"Everything is okay; I got this, love," says Alex.

"Love?" says Coby. I know what you are thinking, Coby got some damn nerve, right? Alex was used to this. You always have the one that got away or the one that you know you can never get back because you fucked up. Jamal looks into Alex's eyes, and rolls up the window. He pulls off, but in his head, he was thinking he never should have left her. He just met her and did not want to step over any boundaries.

"Now back to what I was saying before that clown opened his mouth" says Coby. Alex rolls her eyes and watches Jamal pull off; she was tuning Coby out at this point because she did not know what Jamal thought of her. "You know why I'm here. I want to see my damn daughter," says Coby.

"Now you want to see her after all this time. We have a routine that you will not fuck up for your stupid ass," says Alex. Coby always brought Alex out of character. Alex was very professional and did not like to come out of character especially at her place of business.

It is always a time and a place for the bullshit, but Alex had to let the motherfucker know that she was the same chick, just in a different tax bracket. Coby was getting beside himself, and she had to put him in his place.

"First off, I do not have to answer to you. I will not deny you to see her, but what you will not do is come to a place that has been helping feed *my* daughter for the last ten years while you were playing with hoes and drugs," says Alex.

"Alex," says Coby.

"No, let me finish. You will listen to me as I am talking. I do not answer to you. We are not together and will never be together. You will respect me as Leah's mother because I have been keeping this ship afloat without your raggedy ass," says Alex. Alex put up her finger to the side of Jamal's face. "If you interrupt me one more time, so help me God, it will be your last interruption yet. I will look at my schedule because I am very busy, and I will get with you when I am free," says Alex.

"Who gives a damn about your schedule, Alex?" says Coby.

"Coby, unlike you, I have a job to get back to, and I am not going back and forth with you anymore. Now you can leave, or the police will be called," says Alex. "You are dismissed. I will call you, Coby," says Alex. Alex walks away from Cody to go back into the building as Coby grabs her arm. Alex looks at Cody and breaks away from Coby's grip. Security is now at the door.

"Miss Douglas, is there an issue?" says the security officer.

"This is the reason you cannot see your daughter now," says Alex. Alex breaks away from Coby's grip and walks in the building and gets herself back together on the elevator. Alex's phone gets a text that reads: I KNOW YOU DID NOT REALLY THINK I PULLED OFF, I SAT ACROSS THE STREET. YOU LOOKED AS IF YOU HAD THE SITUATION HANDLED WITH YOUR SEXY ASS. The text was from Jamal. Alex was going to respond to Jamal, but she thought better of it because she was so heated by the shit Coby just pulled.

All Alex could do was think about her daughter as she went back up to her office. She was so embarrassed that Jamal had witnessed that altercation with Coby. Coby was an unstable creature, and that is why Alex has been keeping her distance from him. Coby always knew how to knock Alex off her focus and game since they met. Alex learned how to block out Coby sometimes because she knew that she would never go down that road again. She sat in her office chair and looked at Jamal's text. She could not bring herself to text back right away. Coby has tried to mess up her day, but she had to quickly remind herself who she was and fast. Never let someone get you out of character. Always keep it cute at all times. People will try to make you miserable because they are. Do not fall victim to the bullshit.

Chapter 3

Decisions, Decisions, Decisions

"A lot of people are afraid to say what they want. That's why they don't get what they want."
—Madonna

"Hello" says Michelle, answering the phone.

"Hey boo, I need these edges touched up and a recurl on my hair," says Alex.

"You know I got you," says Michelle.

"When can you take me?" says Alex.

"Girl you know I can fit you in whenever," says Michelle as she laughs.

"Girl, I'm on the way now. I'm wrapping up things from work. we have so much to catch up on," says Alex.

"I bet we do; you always have something new going on," says Michelle.

"We will talk when I get there," as Alex laughs and hangs up the phone. Alex smiles with success in the eyes. *Another day completed in the office* Alex thinks, as she gets up to walk out the door and turn the light off in her soon-to-be old office.

"You can go home, Priscilla; we had a good day today," says Alex.

Alex always lived by a certain motto because she was not raised with a silver spoon in her mouth. Alex had to get it out of the mud, and she did just that. She never let things get to her, and she kept pushing. She stayed late and finished her work in a decent manner. Alex was a bad-ass chick, and she had her life on point to where she could not be stopped. Her five-year goals were reached in three years, and she was not done. She set new goals every year. She murdered her goals every year.

Alex pulls up to Michelle's salon on the corner of 4th and Brunson Streets. Michelle and Alex have known each other for about fifteen years. Michelle's business was booming because she did hair for most of the Boston Celtics' wives, girlfriends, side chicks, baby mommas, and anyone else who needed her services. Michelle's Salon was called 2SLEEKK. The name was inspired by her swag, the way she carried herself.

Michelle had a daughter the same age as Alex's. The girls became friends instantly. Michelle's daughter was named Bria. Alex helped Michelle and vice versa. Alex and Michelle met at a business expo and hit it off from there, Alex was never a friendly person. It was something about Michelle's spirit that drew Alex to Michelle. They have been rocking ever since. They both had visions and dreams.

"Come in, girl; give me like ten minutes" says Michelle.

"Girl, take your time and make these coins," says Alex. Alex sat in one of the other stylist chairs. Michelle's last customer left the shop, and she locked the door.

"Sit in my chair," says Michelle.

"Yes, ma'am," says Alex.

"Tell me, Miss Douglas, what is happening in your world?" says Michelle.

"It is so much; where do I start?" says Alex.

"At this point, anywhere, girl, we have time," says Michelle.

"For starters, Coby called and came past my office with the bullshit the other day. I was just ending my lunch with Jamal. I had to put that fool in his place. To make matters worse, Jamal watched the whole thing from across the street," says Alex.

"Lord, let me get some wine. I know I need some because these players boos or side pieces have gotten on my nerves today," says Michelle.

"Grossman promoted me to Tom's job; sixteenth floor, here I come," says Alex.

Michelle screamed, "Hold up you cannot just slide that in there—Jamal? Who in the hell is Jamal?" says Michelle. "Where did y'all eat lunch, and why is this the first time I am hearing about him?" Alex lowered her head, shaking it. Michelle's mind was so bad.

"Congrats with your promotion, boo; you deserve it. You worked so hard for this opportunity," says Michelle.

"Jamal Stevenson is the man from the Underground who gave me the flower and brought the drinks the other night. He sent flowers to my office and demanded I come to lunch with him," says Alex.

"Oh yes, I do remember his ass," says Michelle.

"He took me to his grandmother's bistro around the corner from my office, but you know I'm not taking these men seriously, girl," says Alex.

"O my goodness, is he that fine-ass man who sent the drinks over?" says Michelle.

"Damn, Chelle, keep up," says Alex as she laughs.

"Okay, I am trying. We are not even going to talk about Coby foolish ass." "He still wants you, and you know it," says Michelle.

"I do not want or need his ass. He showed his ass outside my office," says Alex.

"I can believe it," says Michelle.

"We just share a child," as Alex laughs.

"Ya'll are barely sharing that. Back up a minute—he took you to his granny's spot? Now that's real, girl," says Michelle.

"Yes, he took me to his nana's spot," says Alex.

"You know what that means," says Michelle.

"I just cannot be distracted now with a man; my career is on the up and up," says Alex.

"Alex, chill with that shit damn," says Michelle.

"What? My business is booming; how can I focus on a man?" says Alex.

"Alex, I'm going to keep it real. It has been years since you have been close or even dated anyone," says Michelle.

"What is your point?" says Alex. We as women always get offended when we know our friends are right.

"You need to let loose and get out there. You deserve to be happy," says Michelle.

"Umm hum, I hear you," says Alex.

"That man is fine, and he looks like he has that monnneyy," says Michelle.

"Stop it. You know that I do not need a man with money; that's just a bonus, girl," says Alex.

"I never said you did, boo, but it is a plus," says Michelle. They both laugh but in Alex's head, she was really thinking about it, and Alex started to question herself: *Am I ready to deal with someone right now?*

"Alex, Alex," says Michelle.

"Yeah, what is up?" says Alex. Alex had zoned out and did not even know it.

"Girl, where did you go? I been calling your name, girl," says Michelle?

"My bad, boo. I zoned out for a minute," says Alex.

"I see that," says Michelle.

"Man, my bad, so enough about me, what's is up with you?" says Alex.

"Girl, not much—building as much as I can until Marcus comes home," says Michelle.

"How are you and Marcus doing?" says Alex.

"We are great, you know. I'm ten toes down with that man." says Michelle.

"I know, you are a real one. He is blessed to have you," says Alex.

"I must stand by my man no matter what" says Michelle.

"See that's the love I want, that unconditional hold-you-down type of love" says Alex.

"You can if you give someone a chance. No one is perfect, Alex," says Michelle. Michelle is married, but her husband was doing five years in prison for fraud. He only has a couple more months to go. Alex did not know how she did it, but she held Marcus down like four flat tires. They had a solid marriage, and Michelle's friendship with the girls kept her mind off of his being gone. Michelle never missed a phone call or a visit with her husband.

Alex set herself up to be around positive individuals because people with negative intentions do nothing but try to bring you down with them. All her girls had their own positive things going on, and they were all rooting for each other. As black women, we need friends that are here to encourage you, not tearing each other down, or hating for no reason. Alex and Michelle are still talking, laughing, and sipping on their wine. Alex took her hair seriously because she always got compliments on it, and no one ever touched her hair beside Michelle. There is a knock at the salon door.

Alex looks at Michelle, "Are you expecting someone?" It was Honestie; she was signaling someone to come open the door. Michelle went to the door and opened it to let her in.

"Hey, ladies, I was in the neighborhood, and I saw Alex's car and wanted to see what was going on," says Honestie. Honestie was the life of the party. She always turned the girls up.

"I'm just getting a touch up; you know I have to stay on point," says Alex.

"Yes, I do" says Honestie. Alex phone is ringing, and she looks at both girls.

"Why are you looking at us like that? Who is it?" says Michelle.

"It is that Jamal guy. I do not want to pick it up. I am embarrassed," says Alex.

"Why are you embarrassed?" says Honestie.

"Girl, I will catch you up on tea in a minute," says Michelle.

"Alex, answer the damn phone, and put it on speaker," says Michelle.

"Hello," says Alex.

"Hello, dark chocolate, how are you tonight?" says Jamal.

"I'm good, thanks for asking, and you?" asked Alex.

"What are you up to, and I am great thanks for asking," says Jamal.

"I'm getting my hair done at the moment," says Alex.

"Oh, who are you trying to looking good for? Me I hope," says Jamal.

"Ummm, no sir, for me and my clients," says Alex.

"I was wondering if I could take you out this weekend," says Jamal.

"We just had lunch the other day," says Alex.

"What is your point? That was lunch, and that is in the past," says Jamal. Michelle nudges Alex when Alex looks up. Honestie and Michelle are mouthing for her to go.

"Maybe I want to spend more time with you and get to know you a little more," says Jamal.

"I'll be home in a few. I will let you know what my schedule looks like," says Alex.

"So, are you going to play it like that? Why are you going to fight this?" says Jamal.

"I am not playing anything. I told you I just got promoted today, so I need to finish up some paperwork," says Alex.

"I understand that, sweetheart. I will back off. It is no pressure at all," says Jamal.

"I will call you when I get home if that is okay with you," says Alex.

"Yes, that is fine. I guess I have no choice but to wait," says Jamal.

"Do not act like that," says Alex. Honestie and Michelle are looking at Alex.

"Before I let you off this phone, do you have the cash app?" says Jamal.

"Yes, I do, why?" says Alex.

"No reason, have a nice night, Miss Douglas," says Jamal. Alex hangs up the phone and stares at it.

"Girl, why are you tripping?" says Honestie.

"Why should I open myself up to this man?" says Alex.

"You got a promotion. chick, congrats." says Honestie. "You have cobwebs on your private area; that is why you need to open up to him," says Michelle.

"Shut up, Michelle," says Alex.

"Alex, you need to go. We will watch Leah Beloved; you know she is in good hands," says Michelle.

"Look, finish my hair so I can get home to check on Leah Beloved," says Alex.

"I got you; you are almost done," says Michelle. The girl was talking, and Alex phone dinged. A cash app payment for three hundred dollars came through.

"What the hell?" says Alex. A text followed behind the cash app. SINCE YOU ARE NOT LOOKING GOOD FOR ME, I HOPE YOUR CLIENTS LIKE YOUR HAIR. FROM JAMAL.

"That man is trying to get your attention," says Michelle. Alex texted Jamal back, saying thank you.

The girls wrapped up the conversation and helped Michelle close her shop. They all got into their vehicles and went their separate ways, which really was not that far from each other. All the girls live in the same high-class community, just on separate blocks from each other. Some say that it is weird, but the girls do a lot of things together, and the neighborhood was the safest neighborhood in Boston. As you know, Alex introduced the girls to the neighborhood, of course. Why wouldn't she hook her girls up?

Alex pulls up to her home. This home was laid out with six bedrooms, four bathrooms, and a three-car garage. Some may ask why does she need all those rooms? It was just her and her daughter. The house was 6,000 square feet; her mom had a room when she came into town, and there was a movie room, a guest room, Leah Beloved's room, Alex's room, and her office. When she pulled up into the driveway, all she could do was smile. Alex worked for what she really wanted, and it showed in so many ways.

Alex pulled into the garage and got out the car. She walked through her garage door to her house when she heard laughing coming from the living room of the house. Her daughter and mother are on the couch watching a movie called *Stir Crazy* with Richard Pryor and Gene Wilder.

"Hello, Alex, glad you made it home safe," says Alex mother. Now we must pause for a minute so that I can you about this woman. Mrs. Carmen Hughes was nothing to play with. She was Alex's biggest supporter; she gave her the essentials of life.

Alex did not grow up with a silver spoon in her mouth. She watched her mother grind and make a way for her and her two sisters. Alex was the baby of her siblings; she was spoiled. Her mother raised them to push forward and live outside the box. Alex mother was a single parent as well; now the chick is bad. I know what you are thinking—why was she not there when Alex was in college? She was, but she showed Alex that she had to learn how to balance life, and Alex respected her mother for that. That is why Alex was so disciplined.

Carmen has been married four times. She was always picked on because she got four different men to marry her. Alex and her sisters are amazing women; they turned out so well. Her sisters are Brook and Selene. Brook is a doctor at a leading hospital in Boston, and Selene is also a doctor but of psychology at a different hospital. All the girls were completely different in many ways. Alex never wanted to be a doctor; she wanted to help people in other ways. Alex had to be the black sheep of the family, and she had to go against the grain to be different. She went to the beat of her own drum. Alex did not want to be in anyone's shadow.

Carmen was extremely proud of her daughters despite the fact she could not give them everything when they were younger. "Mom, what are you doing here?" says Alex.

"I sent Stella home, so why do you have to say it like that?" says Carmen. Stella was Alex's housekeeper and nanny from time to time.

"Mom, you know what I mean. You were with Brook last week. What happened?" says Alex.

"She got on my nerves; you know how your sister is," says Carmen. Alex knew her mom was lying, so she texted Brook to get the teas from her because her mother was not going to come clean about what really happened. Carmen was a free spirit. When she wanted to get up and go, she did just that. She spent money how she wanted and traveled how she pleased.

"Why do you always have to think something has happened?" says Carmen.

"Mom, I know you and Brook. Something always happens, Mom," says Alex.

"I got bored, so I made a trip to come see you and my grand-daughter," says Carmen.

"Okay Mom. I hear you. Leah Beloved, it is time to go to bed. You have school tomorrow," says Alex.

"Yes, ma'am," says Leah Beloved.

"Did you do your homework? Let me see it," says Alex.

"It is done, Mom," says Leah Beloved.

"Leah Beloved, I said let me see it," says Alex. Leah Beloved gets up off the couch to get her homework off the table for her mom. Alex looks it over.

"Okay, now go brush your teeth and get in the bed," says Alex. Leah walked upstairs to do what her mother said. "I will be up there in a minute, Leah," says Alex. Alex sat on the couch next to her mom.

"You do not have to talk to her like that," says Carmen.

"Mom, let me parent my child, please; she needs structure. You were worse than that on us," says Alex.

"What is wrong with you? I was not hard on you," says Carmen.

"I had a long day. I got promoted, and Coby came by my job, and I had to put him in his place," says Alex.

"What does he want?" says Carmen?

"He wants to see Leah Beloved," says Alex.

"No, he does not want to see her; he wants to know what you have going on," says Carmen.

"Mom, please, he is still her father," says Alex. As Alex is sitting on the couch, she pulls out her phone to send a text to Jamal.

ARE YOU UP SWEETIE? He texts back, saying yes. She texted him ARE YOU BUSY; CAN I CALL? He texts back NO, I AM NOT BUSY.

"I know that he is, but he is full of it," says Carmen.

"You and I both know that, I am glad you are here. I love you, Mom" says Alex.

"I love you too, baby" says Carmen.

"Mom, I am going up to my room," says Alex.

"Okay baby, goodnight," says Carmen. Alex gets off the couch to walk up the stairs to her room. Alex checks on Leah Beloved in her room. Alex walked in Leah Beloved's room, tucked her in, and kissed her. She stands at Leah's door for a minute and look at her. She heads to her room.

Alex goes in her room and takes off her clothes. Alex gets in the shower; once she is done she oils her body down. She lays cross the bed and calls Jamal. The phone rings.

"Hello?"

"Mr. Stevenson," says Alex.

"Hey dark chocolate, did not think you would call," says Jamal.

"I decided that I will go out with you this weekend but on my terms," says Alex.

"I can go for that, so you like to be in charge or control," says Jamal.

"Maybe I do," says Alex.

"I may let you be in charge if you act right," says Jamal.

"Ha, is that right? What made you send me that money?" says Alex.

"I want you to know how a real man is supposed to treat you," says Jamal. Alex and Jamal talked on the phone all night. Alex lost track of time, and she was enjoying herself. It had been so long since she had been interested in a man. She felt like a kid again. All she did was laugh and talk on the phone with Jamal. They had so much in common. She did not want the conversation to end.

A man like Jamal who is intelligent and sexy gave Alex butterflies. Lord, it is a plus all the way around the board. You have to let a man feed your mind, not just have sexual intercourse with you. A man that can make you think and make you want to better yourself when you already ready are doing good, deserves a hero cookie.

"I feel like a kid again," says Alex.

"I do too," says Jamal.

"I have to work in the morning," says Alex.

"So do I," says Jamal. The conversation continued until 5 a.m. Alex had opened up to Jamal, and she felt good. When a man shows you that he is different, it hits a little different. Relationships are like a car. If you love your car, what do you do? You take care of it, you get it cleaned, and you keep the maintenance done on it. If it's not broke do not fix it.

Chapter 4

Get Up and Go Get It

"Decide ... whether or not the goal is worth the risks involved. If it is, stop worrying."
—Amelia Earhart

"Priscilla, can you pull up my calendar for the rest of the day?" says Alex. Priscilla walks into Alex's office with the iPad and looked at the calendar.

"You have a meeting with Mr. Grossman at 10 o'clock," says Priscilla.

"Okay, can you confirm that meeting?" says Alex.

"Then, Miss Douglas, your calendar is clear for today. You closed that deal early, so nothing else is on the books until next week. I will confirm the meet," says Priscilla.

"Thank you, Priscilla, you can go home early, but you will still get paid for the full day," says Alex.

"Wow, thank you so much, Miss Douglas. Are you feeling okay?" says Priscilla.

"Yes, I am feeling okay, but before you leave, let Mr. Grossman's assistant know I will be up there soon," says Alex.

"I will do that now," says Priscilla.

"Shut the door behind you, please, and have a great day," says Alex.

Alex looks at her phone and calls Jamal. "Hello, how are you today? I hope well. We are going out tonight," says Alex.

"Is that a question or a statement?" says Jamal.

"It is more of a demand; meet me at Shadow La'Pelle 7510 Westwood Lake at 8 p.m.," says Alex.

"Okay, love, I will be there," says Jamal. She hangs up the phone. That's how you do things: you demand what you want. Take action, sometimes, ladies; you do not always have to wait on the man for things. If a man really wants you or wants to date you, he will show up, trust me. If Alex was going to do this, it was going to be on her terms, and the ball was in her court. Alex texted her mother to ask her to pick up Leah Beloved, then her personal stylist Genuva to meet her at her house for some new pieces. Alex then texted the girls in the group chat to tell the girls where she was going and with whom, and it was a 911 emergency to be at her house. A girl's rule states do things on your terms with no pressure. Alex goes to meet Mr. Grossman to see what he wanted.

"Hello, sir," says Alex. "Alex, how are you?" says Grossman.

"I am good; thank you for asking," says Alex.

"I just need you to sign your new contract," says Mr. Grossman. Alex looked over the contract. To her surprise, the terms were amazing.

"Mr. Grossman, this salary is three times more than what I make now," says Alex. "I want to still be in the field as well." All Alex saw was dollar signs when she looked at the contract. She could not believe what she was seeing. She and Leah Beloved would really have a set future.

"If you can handle that too, then go ahead. I will not stop the hustle," says Mr. Grossman.

"Okay great. Thanks, Mr. Grossman, for everything," says Alex.

"I will email you, but the other executives want to have dinner with you to congratulate you on your new position" say Mr. Grossman.

"I am down for that," says Alex. Alex signed the contract and headed back to her old office. Alex walked in her office, closed the door, and screamed. She could not believe that God was blessing her this much.

Alex shut down the office and heads home to meet her stylist. Alex picks up the car phone, and here goes Camilla.

"Hello," says Alex.

You always have that one friend who is a fool and down for you to be wild and do anything.

"No, I am not, girl. I am just going to have dinner with him. That's all—nothing else," says Alex. Alex's phone has an incoming call.

"Hold on, Camilla," says Alex.

"Hello," says Alex. "Hey boo," says Michelle.

"Let me patch you in, Camilla is on the other line" says Alex.

"Camilla," says Alex. "Umm hello, Camilla," says Michelle.

"Hello, Michelle," says Camilla.

"Girl, I cannot believe you are going on this date," say Camilla. "Me neither, but what are you wearing, and do we need to go shopping?" says Michelle.

"Girl, I have no time for shopping. I have Genuva on the way to the house as we speak," says Alex.

"I forgot Mrs. Big Time that you have a personal stylist and what not," says Michelle as she laughs.

"Well, I am on the way to your house now," says Camilla.

"So am I. Is the door code still the same?" says Michelle.

"Yes, it is, but why are y'all on the way to my house? It is just a date. You're all tripping," says Alex. Camilla and Michelle never answered her question; they both hung up their phones. Alex looked at her phone and tossed her phone in the passenger seat. Alex rolls her eyes and turns up her music and heads home. Alex pulls up to her house to see both ladies were already there, blocking her driveway. Alex got out the car and walked into her house to be greeted by the girls and Genuva, making all this noise.

"All you heifers did not have to hang up on me. Hey, Genuva," says Alex.

"Hello, Miss Douglas," says Genuva.

"Well, Miss Douglas, what type of look are you looking for tonight?" says Genuva.

"Genuva, I told you to call me Alex. We have been working together too long for you to be formal, hun," says Alex.

"Yes, ma'am," says Genuva. "Stop with that," says Alex as she laughs.

"Okay, okay. I have a couple of sexy options," says Genuva.

"Let's see what you have," says Alex.

"Alex, try on that black Gucci dress," says Michelle.

"No, try on that blue Louie dress," says Camilla.

"Can both of y'all let the person I am paying do this, please?" says Alex.

"No, we cannot; that is what we are here for," says Michelle as she laughs.

"They have a point," says Genuva. Camilla laughs and sips the wine she is drinking.

"Y'all can both shut up, and where did you get wine?" says Alex.

"Your refrigerator. Your mom said I could have some," says Camilla. Michelle's phone rings, and it is Honestie; she gives her the rundown of what is going on. Michelle hangs up the phone.

"Honestie says she is on the way," says Michelle.

"Okay, it's a party now" says Camilla.

"No, it is not, and sit your ass down, girl," says Alex as she laughs.

"I am going to enjoy myself," says Camilla.

"No one invited y'all over her," says Alex.

"Since when we need an invite, sis?" says Camilla.

"Can someone get me some wine?" says Alex.

"It is right there," says Michelle. Alex rolls her eyes at both girls and pours herself some wine as well.

"Would you like some wine, Genuva," says Alex?

"Yes, I would," says Genuva.

Alex started to try on many outfits, with the girls looking and commenting on the outfits.

"Hello, ladies," says Honestie as she dances into the room.

"All I'm going to say is you better slay, sis," says Honestie.

"Alex this dress just came in yesterday, try this on," says Genuva. Leah walks into the room to greet her mom.

"How was your day, baby?" says Alex.

"Hey aunties," says Leah. "My day was good, Mom, but yours looks like it is about to get started."

Camilla laughed; she was getting tipsy, so everything was funny to her.

"Yes, Leah I am going out," says Alex.

"Okay, Mom, is it okay that I stay up with nana tonight?" says Leah.

"Yes, "says Alex. "Go get your nana for me, please," says Alex.

"She is getting so big," says Honestie.

"Girl, I know. That means I am getting old," says Alex.

"No, ma'am, that means you are getting wise, hun. Correct that, we are getting better with age," says Michelle.

"I know that's right, chick. I'm at my prime," says Camilla. All the girls laugh and sip their wine, while Alex weighs her options with her outfits. Alex decided to go with the red body dress and the black red bottom heels.

"Genuva, you are a genius," says Alex.

"The color red is a loud and bold color; it makes you stand out, and you are definitely noticed without saying one word if you are wearing it right, Believe that."

"Okay, sis, you better slay," says Michelle. Alex turns around to let each girl see the dress.

"Damn, Alex, that dress is really showing that ass," says Camilla. Alex bends over and twerks in the dress.

"I have been working out," says Alex.

Girl I see says Honestie.

"I'm about to take a shower, y'all," says Alex. The girls continued to talk as Alex took a shower and oiled her body down with coconut oil. Alex believed in a healthy life and skin, and she worked out in her spare time when she could. Aromatherapy was her thing, mainly.

"Alex, hunny, you wanted me," says Carmen. Yes, I do, Mom. Do not have Leah up too late, eating all that stuff," says Alex.

"I'm grown; do not tell me what I can and cannot do with my grandchild," says Carmen.

"Mom, come on, for real," says Alex.

"Look, do not worry about us. You need to go get that ass tapped," says Carmen. Michelle looks up from her phone and laughs.

"Mom, really, are your serious right now?" says Alex.

We all know that you have had no sex since Harriette Tubman set slaves to freedom says Carmen. All the girls laughed so hard at Alex's mom.

Mom you can go, all of you all can go say Alex.

"Oh, so you're mad now," says Camilla.

"No, I'm not mad. I know my car will be here soon," says Alex.

"Alex, enjoy yourself," says Carmen.

Alex finished getting dressed, and the girls left. Alex heads downstairs and kisses Leah on the forehead, saying, "Be good for your nana." "Mom, you be safe."

"Nana and I are good," says Leah.

"Thank you, baby, I love you. Mom, remember what I said," says Alex.

"No, you remember what I said," says Carmen, as she laughs. Alex walks out her front door and is greeted by her driver. Alex stepped into the car.

"Hey, Joe," says Alex.

"Hello Miss Douglas, where are we going tonight?" says Joe.

"Take me to Shadow La'Pelle 7510 Westwood Lake," says Alex. As Alex rides to the restaurant, she is going back and forth with her thoughts. She almost turned around and went back home, but something told her to go. Alex has not been in the dating world for some time.

She has been so life and career driven that she just left dating alone. Her focus was Leah Beloved and her wellbeing. Alex is not the type of chick to take care of any man, period, or be taken care of. Alex's mother always told her a man is a plus. Never depend on him for anything. Always make your own bag. What he gives you, save it. Alex had a motto that she went by. It was simple: you must bring something to the table besides penis and headaches. Alex's plate was full for her to add more to it, you had to be special. Hell, it is damn near a feast when you look at it. Alex was in her bag, a great mother and friend, and was driven. Before Alex knew it, she was pulling up to Shadow La'Pelle. Alex was always deep in her thoughts all the time, she was such an overthinker.

The driver pulled in front of the restaurant and opened Alex's door. "Have fun, Miss Douglas," says Joe the driver. When she stepped out the car, those oiled legs shined in her Louis Vuitton stilettos. Alex had this red dress that hugged her body so well, she had the walk of a goddess. The lights to the outside of the restaurant were so pretty, they glistened in the dark. As her hips switched from side to side, one foot in front of the other, Alex walked with the most confidence that she had. Alex walked into the restaurant to be greeted by the host. I am Alexandria Douglas. I have a reservation for two," says Alex.

"Ma'am the other party is here already, follow me I will take you to the room" says the host.

"Wait, the room? What room? I did not book a room," says Alex.

"The gentlemen with you did," say the hostess.

"We should not be in a room," says Alex with a confused voice.

"The gentleman bought the back room when he arrived," says the hostess.

Alex could only smile and follow behind the host. Alex's mind was blown, and all she wanted to do was text the girls. When the hostess opened the backroom door, Jamal had a bunch of roses for her on the table. Alex walked in. Jamal was on the phone, and he could not finish his sentence when she walked in because his eyes were locked on her. He instantly hung up the phone and stood up to greet her with a hug.

"Hello, Jamal," says Alex.

"Hello, Alex, I hope this is nice enough for you," says Jamal.

"You had to take control of the situation, didn't you, but I like it," says Alex.

"You thought I was going to let you one up me? No, you have met your match," says Jamal.

"This was my idea, and it is not a competition, but I like how you took control," says Alex. Jamal laughs and pulls her chair out, so she can sit down.

"I never said it was a competition sweetie. You deserve to be treated like the queen you are," says Jamal. Jamal goes around the table to sit in his chair.

"Thank you for the flowers. I am starting to think you own a flower shop," says Alex with a smile on her face.

"It was my pleasure. I do not own one, but my aunt does own a flower shop," says Jamal. The waitress walks in with a bottle of Dom Perignon. The waitress pops the cork, pours Alex a glass, and then Jamal.

"Can I help you with anything else?" says the waitress.,

"Let us look over the menu and I will call you back in, in a minute," says Jamal. Jamal had this deep ass sexy voice that made you just want to jump down his throat. "I must say that you look amazing, I cannot stop looking at you" says Jamal.

"Thank you, love, and you do not look bad yourself," says Alex. Alex knew Jamal looked dead gorgeous, and the way he smelled could make you wet.

Alex could not tell him how good he looked because it would make her seem vulnerable, which, ladies, is not true. Let that man know how you feel, that you are feeling him. A closed mouth does not get fed.

"Alex, you intrigue me, the way you present yourself," says Jamal. Alex smiles and put her hair behind her ear. The waiter came back out to refill their glasses and take their orders. "Are you ready to order, darling?" says Jamal. Jamal had this demeanor about him; he was to cool for school. Jamal was a manly man; you can tell that he took charge. This man was so smooth but right on point. Alex knew that Jamal was different, but everything in her gut told her not to trust him. Ladies, this is a defense mechanism that we use to protect ourselves and heart. Alex was tired of being disappointed. She had a wall up that was like the great wall of China. "Yes, I'm ready to order," says Alex.

"You go first sweetie" says Jamal.

"Okay I would like the T-bone steak well done, the roasted potatoes, broccoli and cheese, and a house salad with ranch dressing," says Alex. Jamal looked at Alex and started to smile at her. Jamal knew inside that this woman was for him.

"What would you like, sir"" says the waitress.

"I would like the T-bone steak. medium rare, and the linguine pasta shrimp, with the loaded potatoes," says Jamal.

"I will be back with your house salad and some bread," says the waitress.

"Thank you," says Jamal.

"You are welcome, sir," says the waitress. The waitress walks away, but she is staring at Jamal and was about to run into the door.

"You have an admirer," says Alex. Jamal looks back and laughs. "What made you get a room" says Alex?

"I wanted to be alone with you without other distractions. To tell me about yourself more," says Jamal.

"What do you want to know?" says Alex.

"Everything," says Jamal.

Ladies, when a man wants you to really know him, you can decipher whether he is genuine or not. At that very moment, Alex got shy and started to smile and put her hair behind her ear again. Alex could not resist, she wanted to be all in with Jamal, but she just kept hearing in her head *Take it slow, dummy.* Alex's mind quickly went left, she could not stop having thoughts in her about her and Jamal making passionate love all night. Alex's thoughts were interrupted by her phone ringing.

"Hello," says Alex.

"How is the date going sis?" says Camilla.

"I will call you later. and do not call me anymore." says Alex as she tries hangs up the phone.

All the girls start to speak at one time. "Well. you have to call all of us; we will be waiting" says Camilla.

"Hey, girl," says Honestie.

"Hey, boo," says Michelle.

"Are y'all still together? Y'all need a life. Goodbye," says Alex. Alex hung the phone up and put it on silent.

"You know you do not have to do that," say Jamal.

"Yes, I do. You don't understand; my friends are crazy," says Alex.

"It is good you have friends that check on you, sweetie," says Jamal. "So back to what I want to know about you, and do not change the subject again," says Jamal.

"I will not tell you everything, just a little information for this first date," says Alex.

"Why is that, Alex? Why are you afraid?" says Jamal.

"I am not afraid. You always have to leave some things as a mystery," says Alex.

"A mystery, huh?" says Jamal.

Before Alex could answer Jamal, the waitress came out with their food. You could still see the steam coming off of the food.

"This looks good. I am so hungry," says Alex.

"Did you work through lunch again?" says Jamal. Alex knew she couldn't tell Jamal that she left work early, had her personal stylist come by to get the right outfit, and converse with the girls before coming to meet him. She knew he would get the big head, and that cannot happen just yet.

"Yes, I worked through lunch. I am listing new properties, and with my new promotion, it is an adjustment," says Alex.

"I understand. I have a big case coming up that is stressing me out," says Jamal.

"Stress? What type of lawyer are you?" says Alex.

As you can see. Alex has totally changed the subject because she was not ready to give Jamal many details about her life. Alex was not sure if she could open up to Jamal because she had always been told she was too strong of woman. She could not have a man take her there or even down that road so early. Why was she resisting? Why did she feel this way? This man made her feel so comfortable, though. The other half of her was saying girl let go

She wondered: *How long has it been since someone has caressed my body?* Alex could only imagine what type of skills Jamal had. *Look at his arms for goodness sake. At any rate, let me get out of my thoughts. I am on a date, girl, so get back to that man who is in front of you, trying to see through your clothes.* Jamal had this seductive look on his face that made Alex clinch her thighs. The tension between these two was so high.

"I am a defense lawyer," says Jamal.

"Oh, okay, so you get the bad guys off," says Alex as she laughs.

"Not necessarily all time but mostly," says Jamal as he laughs.

"That is interesting," says Alex.

"I do deal with high-profile cases I cannot get into the specifics of," says Jamal.

"I understand that; you are an important man," says Alex.

"I just make it hard for the other lawyer; just know that," says Jamal.

"I see that you're just saying you're good at your job," says Alex.

"You could say that. That's why they pay me the big bucks," says Jamal.

"Well, I like that," says Alex.

"I know I keep saying this, but you look amazing. Are you mixed with anything?" says Jamal. Why do people think you always have to be mixed with some other race? Black is beautiful, people.

"Lord, noooooo. I'm fully black, sweetheart, and the naps on the back of my neck show it if I do not go see Michelle for my regular appointments," says Alex. Jamal laughed and cut into his steak. The two talked and ate. They were the last two in the restaurant. The waitress came over into the room.

"Hello, we are now closed," says the waitress. Alex and Jamal looked at each other; neither one wanted to depart from the other. They both left the restaurant and went their separate ways.

Chapter 5

A Night to Remember

*"Once you figure out what respect tastes like, it tastes
better than attention."*
—Pink

arilyn Monroe once said, "I'm selfish, impatient and a little insecure. I make mistakes, I am out of control and at times hard to handle. But if you can't handle me at my worst, then you sure as hell don't deserve me at my best." We all want love in some way, shape, or form even if we do not admit it. No one wants to be by themselves like the old lady with twenty-seven cats. Love will find you; you have to be patient. You cannot rush your forever thing. I need some things to marinate with you for a moment. This is date number five for these two. Alex liked Jamal because he was up to trying new things. He knew some great eating places, and the conversation was always great. Jamal and Alex were at The Palm Boston, a hot new restaurant they had both wanted to try.

"The night is still young, and we both do not want to end this," says Jamal.

"You must speak for yourself. How do you know I do not have another date waiting on me?" says Alex jokingly.

"You and I feel this connection between us, so I know there is no one else," says Jamal.

"You are just that confident," says Alex.

"I actually am," says Jamal. As Alex could see, Jamal was used to getting his way and is always being told yes.

Now, ladies, pay close attention to this tea I'm about to give you. To the men reading this, I'm sorry but I have to put my ladies up on game, but you can probably use this as well, so sit back and keep reading. At this very moment, Alex has to realize what she needs to do as far as deciding which will see how this night will go. A girl's rule clearly states that Alex was either going to (1) let him chase her which he was doing a good job of so far, or (2) give the yes he was looking for and enjoy her night with him. If you want a good time, pick option B. It is okay to let the man have his way sometimes, ladies.

Decisions, decisions, decisions. Jamal interrupts her thoughts with his fine ass. "Do you want desert, ma'am? They have the best crème brule in town," says Jamal.

"Look at you, like you know what you are talking about," says Alex.

"I do, baby; also I know the head chef," says Jamal. Alex decided to be grown and let the night unfold like it may. She needed to let her hair down, and it was the weekend, so why not? She figured what does she really have to lose because her and Jamal had a vibe.

"You know the Underground is supposed to be jumping tonight, celebrating their ten-year anniversary. You want to slide over there after desert?" says Jamal.

"I do not mind," says Alex.

"Some homeboys of mine are going to be there. Text your friends and tell them to come out," says Jamal. Alex was in the mood to hear music and tweak a little bit to celebrate her new promotion, which she still had not celebrated.

"Let me text my girls to see if they want to slide, but one is married and the other is engaged," says Alex.

"That's fine; it is just adults having fun," says Jamal. She picked up her phone and sent the text to the girls in a group chat. Of course, as you know, Camilla was the first one to respond, but everyone else followed suit after her. Alex looked up from her phone at Jamal.

"Sure, we can go, I am in the mood for some music tonight, and the girls are ready for this turn-up," says Alex.

As the waitress came back to check on them, she asked, "Would you all like anything else?"

"Can we get desert?" says Jamal.

"What will it be, sir," says the waitress?

"We are going to each get the crème brule," says Jamal.

"Great choice, I will be right back," says the waitress.

"Baby, do you want anything else?" says Jamal.

"No sweetie. I'm good. Thanks for getting me my own. I did not want to share," says Alex.

"I did not want to share, either. We are going to have fun tonight," says Jamal. Alex and Jamal laughed. Alex smiled at Jamal because she saw so much good in his eyes.

"Is that right?" said Alex. As Jamal and Alex were talking about their day, the waitress brought the deserts and the check back to the table. Alex and Jamal both pulled out their black cards and looked at each other.

"What are you doing? You can put your card up now," says Alex.

"No, I will not put my card away. I've got this," says Jamal.

"It was my date this time, so I have this. Put your coins away. You already tried to take over once; I refuse for a fifth time," says Alex.

"I will not argue with you" says Jamal. Alex gave the waitress her card and ate her desert.

"You do not always have to pick up the check," says Alex.

"Yes, I do," says Jamal.

"How do you figure that?" says Alex as she scoops her desert.

"You have been footing the bill for a while; let me now take the lead. Also, how does it taste?" says Jamal.

"It is good and smooth; thank you for being so sweet" says Alex. All Alex could do was think of how Jamal tastes if you want to be clear. Ladies, have you ever thought about taking out sex in an equation? Do not beat me up; hear me out. Nowadays no one dates, it is just sex and that's it. Alex and Jamal have been on five dates. That does not seem like a lot, but they both have busy schedules. Take out the penis and just get to know someone. You will see their real intentions for you. The waitress brought Alex's card back to the table.

"This is your copy, and this is my copy," says the waitress.

"Thank you, you were great," said Alex.

"This is for your troubles," says Jamal. Jamal gave the waitress a two-hundred-dollar tip.

Thank you all so much," says the waitress.

"You're welcome," says Jamal.

As they both got up to head to the door, the hostess said, "Your car will be around, Mr. Stevenson."

"Thank you," says Jamal.

"Can you bring my car around as well?" says Alex.

"No need for that. I told you driver that he could go home for the night and paid him for the rest of the night," says Jamal.

"When did you do that" says Alex.

"I have connections; that is nothing you need to worry about," says Jamal.

"Let me pay you back," says Alex.

"No Alex. It is taken care of; just enjoy the night," says Jamal. The door man held the door for the both of them as they walked out the door and entered Jamal's town car. All Alex could think of was that this man is just full of surprises. She was not used to being treated so well by a man, as you can see. Alex was used to being the dominant one. She did not really know how to take orders, especially not from a man. It felt so good for a man to treat her so well. Alex's phone rang.

"Yes, what's up?" says Alex.

"Where are you chick? We are here," says Michelle.

"We are on the way now," says Alex.

"Hurry up; you better tell me everything when you get here," says Michelle.

"Girl, goodbye," says Alex as she laughs. They both got into the town car, and the driver closed the door.

"You like control, don't you," says Jamal. Alex looked at him with the most seductive eyes and leaned over as she whispered in his perfectly shaped ear.

"Always," says Alex. Jamal reached over and kissed Alex on her soft lips. They were tonguing each other down when they pulled up to the Underground. They stopped kissing and got out of the town car. Alex and Jamal walked through the door of the Underground, and it seemed as if everyone was having a good time. They walked to the VIP section and met Jamal's friends.

Alex texted the GroupMe with the girls for them to come to the VIP section near the stage. When Alex and Jamal got to the VIP section, Jamal's homeboys were already drinking and turned-up. Jamal dapped up all his homeboys and introduced Alex to the guys.

"Baby, these are the guys," said Jamal. Derek was a football player, Terrance was a lawyer, Michael was a contractor for his own company, and Thomas was a doctor. His friends were no scrubs. There was so much black excellence in the room. They all nudged each other when Alex turned around to look in the crowd. You know, all men have that signal they do to each other.

"How did you find her?" says Michael, as he yells over the music.

"Man, chill. I will talk to you about it later," says Jamal.

"No, I'm serious, man," says Michael.

"We will talk later, man," said Jamal. Jamal was not a kiss-and-tell type of guy. He kept his business private.

"Okay, I was just playing, but calm down," says Thomas.

"I'm calm; I just really am feeling her," says Jamal. Alex sees the girls, and she waves them over to the VIP section.

"What would you drink, baby," says Jamal as he grabs Alex's waist and whispers in her ear. Alex was not a drinker because she never knew how to hold her liquor well. She did drink wine, though; it was very classy and more her speed. She left the hard stuff to the professionals like Hennessey; it puts hair on your chest. *Wait, did Jamal just call me baby again? Look at him, I mean, I do make these impressions on people. He is going to make me get a big head, and my head does not need to be any bigger. He is calling me baby; maybe it does not mean anything. Alex, relax and enjoy your night.*

"I just want some chardonnay, love," says Alex. The girls walked into the VIP section. Everyone introduced themselves, and the party began.

The bottles started to fly, everyone was showing off and dancing to the music. Alex ordered some wings because she started to get tipsy, which gave her the munchies. She was finally enjoying herself and was not ready for this night to end.

"Are you okay, baby?" says Jamal.

"Yes, I'm okay, just a little tipsy," says Alex as she laughs.

"Oh, Lord," says Jamal. Alex got up to join the girls, they were twerking and turned up.

"Are you girls having fun?" says Alex.

"Yes, thank you girl for thinking of us," says Honestie. Alex walks over to dance with Jamal. Jamal admired Alex's body and placed his hands on her hips and caressed her ass. For the first time in a while, she felt so free. She did not care what people thought about her. On top of that, the night was going so well.

"I like your friends; they really know how to turn-up" says Jamal.

"I like your friends as well. I cannot believe that you know Boston's top quarterback. My mom would go crazy if she knew I was in VIP with him," says Alex.

"Yes, we have been friends since we were seven. He is my right hand. So your mom is a football fan," says Jamal.

"She is a huge fan; we all are football fans," says Alex. She just kept thinking to herself that she and Jamal have a lot in common, and it was way too good to be true.

Something had to be wrong with this man, and only time would tell. Ladies, we will talk ourselves out of a good thing, won't we? Alex always looked at the bad in a situation before she saw the good; that was just how she was. Alex knew that was her problem, and she did not have the slightest clue on how to fix it because she had been like that for so long. Alex and Jamal were in their own zones, vibing out when a red chick walked over to the VIP section. She stood on the outside and signaled Jamal to come over. Alex looked at the girls, and they knew what that meant. The look means be on high alert and pay attention, just in case it is some foolishness.

All Alex could think was *Here we go. I told you something was not right.* Jamal excused himself and told Alex he would be right back. Alex could see was the chick waving her hands in Jamal's face and rolling her neck. The first rule of being a boss chick is never let the next chick see you sweat or think you have pressure. The reason is because you do not know the situation at hand. Alex got up from the couch walked over to the girls because she knew they had something to say. Alex wanted to get that over with because she was tipsy and would not have time for this later.

"Who is that?" asked Honestie.

"If I knew I would tell you," says Alex.

"Ain't no pressure though," says Camilla. Camilla is that friend who is always ready to jump or pop off. No matter how successful she gets, she will still show out when it comes to her girls.

"Calm down. There will be none of that tonight; we are having a good time," says Alex.

"You know how she is, and she has had a couple of drinks too," says Michelle.

"Trust me I know," says Alex.

"As long as she keeps it cute, we will be okay," says Camilla. The girls all said that part at the same time and laughed. Alex walks over to the bottle of wine and pours herself another glass. Jamal ends the conversation with the mysterious woman and walks away. He walks over to Alex to see if she is okay and to try to explain himself. Alex cuts Jamal off. Yes, she wanted to know who this woman was, but there was a time and a place for it.

"Baby, we need to talk," says Jamal.

"We will, but can you go get my wings from the kitchen?" says Alex. Jamal stepped away to get Alex's food and the red-boned woman returns.

"Hey, you chick," says the red-boned woman to Alex. Camilla saw what was going on and was turned-up already. Camilla somehow heard the chick over the music, trying to get Alex's attention. Before Alex could respond, Camilla was walking over to the woman and her. "How can I help you?" says Camilla.

"You cannot help me because I am not talking to you," says the red-boned woman.

"I'm talking to you though," says Camilla.

"I do not see why; can her black ass not talk for herself?" says the red-boned woman.

Now pause for a cause; do not get things twisted. Alex can hold her own, and she will bust a grape in a fruit fight. Camilla knew Alex had too much to lose, and Camilla already had a reputation for not caring at all. Alex steps in front of Camilla because she knew what her next move was going to be.

"I can talk for myself, but I do not argue with the someone who is not important or disrespectful," says Alex.

As I told you before Alex and Camilla grew up together. The two of them have been in many fights because of Camilla's slick-ass mouth. They were grown now, and that was not always the solution. They both knew that this situation had to be handled differently and accordingly. Alex turns to Camilla and gives her the pipe down look.

"I can talk for myself. Camilla, relax," says Alex.

"Disrespectful?" says the red-boned woman?

"Yes, you heard what I said," says Alex.

"Alex, you better handle it, or I will," says Camilla. Camilla steps back to give Alex the floor.

"I am Alexandria Douglas. If you want to speak, we can do that, but I will not make a scene in here, love," says Alex. Michelle and Honestie walked over to see what are going on.

"Your friends do not need to come over here," says the red-boned woman.

"Nothing is going to happen to you," says Alex. Ladies, remember this: never hop out of character. To get respect you have to give it, and that's from anyone who deserves it. Alex demanded it from anyone, and that was a fact.

"Okay, Miss Douglas, you need to watch your back," says the red-boned chick.

"Why would I do something like that?" says Alex.

"If you know what I know, you would steer clear because Jamal is mine," says the red-boned chick.

"Oh, is that right? Well, sweetheart, when I am done, I may give him back because apparently Jamal did not get that memo," says Alex. Alex had a slick-ass mouth as well and never took any type of shit from the next person. Jamal was not giving baby girl any play, so Alex was not worried about the chick. Jamal was so busy talking to the owner that he did not see what was happening between Alex and the red-boned chick. Camilla's eyes just kept getting bigger and bigger because she wanted to say something so badly. She knew Alex was okay and had things handled, but she was not leaving Alex's side.

For the books, never ever let your real friend get caught slipping. Jamal walks back over the VIP section with Alex's wings. He saw the chick. "Why are you still here?" says Jamal.

"You know why," says the red-boned chick.

"This here is my woman. I do not want you," says Jamal as he points to Alex. Jamal looks at the woman and points her to the door. Alex laughed at the woman and waves her goodbye. You can have a petty moment or two. Alex was just shocked that Jamal did that.

Alex told Camilla to brush it off and walk away. "Have fun, boo; it's over," says Alex.

"I am good; people just always try to make themselves seem more relevant than a little bit," says Camilla. The red-boned chick walks away from the VIP section and heads toward the exit of the club. Jamal pulls Alex to the side to explain again to Alex what happened with the red-boned chick.

"Baby, follow me," says Jamal. Alex and Jamal head out the VIP to a quiet area in the back of the club.

"I need to apologize for what just happened. I do not even play these games," says Jamal.

"What is going on, Jamal? I do not do drama," says Alex.

"She was a client of mine who got attached for no reason. I do not mix business with pleasure," says Jamal.

"Jamal are you sure," says Alex.

"I have no reason to lie to you. She has been on my trail ever since," says Jamal. Alex looked into Jamal's eyes, and he appeared to be sincere. Alex kissed Jamal, as the issue was dead in her eyes.

"I got it. Thank you for explaining this to me," says Alex.

"I do not want to lose you or cause you any harm, emotional or physically," says Jamal.

Alex enjoyed her night with Jamal and her friends. It was hitting 2 a.m., and Alex was ready to go. She had not been out in a while, so her body was getting tired. Alex leaned over to Jamal and whispered in his ear, "I am ready to go, sweetie."

"Okay, anything you want," says Jamal. Alex did not know that Jamal meant just what he said. Alex said bye to the girls, and she and Jamal walked toward the door. Alex's phone vibrated, and she looked down at her phone. It was Camilla with a text. TEXT ME WHEN YOU GET TO YOUR DESTINATION OR WHEREVER YOU'RE GOING. Alex texted back OKAY and followed Jamal. When Alex and Jamal got outside, his town car was already out front. Jamal grabbed her hand and escorted her into the car. Jamal walked around the car to get in on the other side. He got in the car and shut the door.

"Oscar, can you take Miss Douglas home?" says Jamal.

"Yes sir, what is the address, Miss Douglas?" says Oscar. Alex looks over at Jamal and gives him a look.

"How do you know that I want to end the night or go home?" says Alex

"Alex, I know you are tipsy, and I do not want you to do this because of that," say Jamal.

"I am a big girl, Jamal, and I am in my right mind," says Alex. Jamal looked at Alex and yes, he wanted her in every way shape and form. He just was not sure what to do, so he did what any man would do.

"Oscar, head to the house," says Jamal.

"Yes, sir," says Oscar. Alex looked out the window and thought to herself. *I do need to go home,* she thought to herself. Alex knew she had not been touched by a man in so long—a real man, that is. Alex texted the girls in the group chat and let them know where she was going. To her surprise she only received a text back saying, BE SAFE AND YOU GO BOO. All she could do was smile and put her phone back in her Chanel bag. Your girls will not block when you need that ass tapped right, trust that.

"Baby I have to tell you something," says Jamal.

"What's that?" says Alex.

"I was engaged two years ago, but it did not work out," says Jamal.

"Wow, what happened—if you don't mind me asking?" says Alex.

"I don't mind; that is why I am telling you. We were deeply in love. She got pregnant and aborted my child and did not tell me until weeks later. I loved her so much that I tried to forgive her. In my healing process, she cheated on me" says Jamal. Alex looked at Jamal.

"Do you still love her?" says Alex.

"No, that ship sailed a long time ago," says Jamal.

"I am sorry, Jamal," says Alex as she looked into his eyes.

"What are you sorry for?" says Jamal.

"That it happened to you," says Alex.

"No need to be sorry, love; it is life. We win some, and we lose some," says Jamal.

The drive was not long, getting to Jamal's house from the club. Alex was so into her thoughts that she did not know the car had stopped. When they pulled up to his house, Alex was in shock. This had been the house that she adored. She has driven past it plenty of times because she sold other houses in the area. This was her dream home. Oscar opened the door for Alex. "Are you okay, baby?" says Jamal.

"Yes, I am. You would not believe me if I told you," says Alex. Alex stepped out of the car, and Jamal laughed.

"Tell me what you have to tell me," says Jamal. Alex and Jamal walked up to the door, and he opened it. Alex walked through the door, and her eyes got so big.

"Who is your interior designer?" saying Alex.

"I'll get you the number in the morning. Would you like some wine?" says Jamal.

"Yes, I would." says Alex.

"Marta, can you pour my guest a glass of wine?" says Jamal.

"Yes sir, Mr. Stevenson," says Marta.

"Bring it up to the suite," says Jamal.

"Alex, you can take off your shoes and put on those slippers. I know your feet are tired," says Jamal. Alex looked down at the white slippers on the floor.

"You have slippers for all your guests?" says Alex.

"Why do you want to start with me?" says Jamal. Alex took off her red bottoms and slipped on the slippers.

"Wow, these slippers feel good," says Alex.

"They are imported from Asia," says Jamal. Alex and Jamal got on the elevator and took it up to the suite.

"All this house for one person," says Alex. Alex and Jamal got off the elevator. Jamal grabbed Alex's hand and took her to the master suite. Alex walked over to the bed and sat down.

"Is it okay if I take a shower?" says Jamal.

"Sure," says Alex.

"You can get comfortable; I won't bite unless you want me to," say Jamal. He laughs and walks into the bathroom. Alex laughed and watched Jamal walk into the bathroom. Alex hears a knock at the door.

"Come in," says Alex.

"Hello, Miss Douglas. Here is your wine," says Marta.

"Aww, thank you," says Alex. Marta leaves and shuts the door. Alex sips her wine and sits back on the bed. She wonders whether she should go in the bathroom with Jamal. The first thing she thought about was what every woman thinks: *should I get these bundles wet?* Do not judge us, we love our hair. *Lord, Michelle is going to kill me, but this curl is meant to get wet, so let's try it out. Michelle will just congratulate me because I finally got some good, but I do not know if it is good or not. Jamal is in that bathroom naked or getting naked, and I am out here debating whether or not to join him.*

Alex needed stop thinking about her hair and go in that bathroom. That is what she really came over here for. Her body aching from a long day. Alex begins to unzip her dress and pulls it down. She unsnaps her lace bra and pulls the straps over her arms, dropping it to the floor. Silently her lace thong fell to the floor. Alex walks toward the bathroom. As she steps into the bathroom. She stares at Jamal in the steaming shower. All she could think about is, *Is this man going to tear me to pieces?* She was ready. Jamal's frame was muscular, like a page out of GQ magazine. Alex stood and admired his body as the water rolled down his head to his glistening six pack right before touching his legs and feet. Jamal did not see her because his back was turned toward the door. Alex opened the shower door and rubbed her soft hands down Jamal's back, leaning in closer to kiss and caress his back. The marble floor was heated. Jamal turns around with satisfaction in his eyes and begins kissing Alex. He grabs the shower door and shuts it. Their bodies meet and Jamal instantly gets hard. Her robust breast touched his cutup chest.

"Baby are you sure about this?" says Jamal. Jamal pinned her up against the wall. Alex wrapped her legs around his waist.

"I would not be here if I wasn't ready," says Alex as she whispers in Jamal's ear.

"I want all of you," says Jamal. Jamal kisses Alex's breast as his tongue goes around each one of her breasts.

Alex was wide open at this point; there was no turning back.

"I do not know if I can do that, baby," says Alex as she moans. If she was wrong, she wanted to be wrong with Jamal, as the water glistened down both of their chocolate bodies. The steam in the shower was so thick you could barely see inside the shower. Alex hair was dripping wet.

"Alex, I got you," says Jamal. Jamal lifted Alex just enough to slide is ten-inch penis in her perfectly shaped vagina. Jamal was in a squatting position, and his feet were planted. Beginning to stroke her passionately and kiss all over her sexy breasts, Jamal sucked on Alex's neck. Arousing her areola, Alex stops Jamal. She felt herself about to come. Jamal pinned her back up against the wall.

"Baby, give it to me," says Jamal. Alex's legs got so weak. Jamal made sure he had a good grip on Alex's ass. You would really want to be a fly on the wall. Ahhhhhh, is all you could hear as Jamal thrusted Alex up and down on the slippery wall. Jamal had to catch his breath because the steam was getting into his lungs. You could hear "Motivation" by Kelly Rowland playing in the background. Alex was taking every inch of it like a champ. Alex was weak, and Jamal was hitting every possible spot. As her freshly manicured nails dug into Jamal's firm cut muscular back, he said "Damn, baby."

"Sorry, baby, I cannot help it" says Alex. Alex started to call Jamal's name over and over. Jamal moaned because he could not believe how tight Alex was. Her vagina gripped his penis like a glove. Jamal went harder and faster, so Alex could come again. Alex almost slipped up and said I love you; she had to catch herself. Before you say anything or judge her, yes it was that good. It was the best sex she had ever had. Alex did not have sexual contact with many men.

The friction from both of their bodies was unbelievable; the chemistry definitely there. Jamal was mesmerized by Alex's body, as he caressed it. Jamal rubbed and gripped her ass. Jamal lowered Alex's legs to the floor. He turned her around and started to kiss her from her neck to her back. Alex moaned because Jamal got lower and lower. *Oh my God* is all that Alex could think. Jamal got on his knees and went to work. Jamal lifted up and lightly bit her slightly above her hip. Jamal then went back down and slid his tongue back and forth inside Alex's clit. "Fuck," says Alex. Jamal's tongue was like a whirlwind, just going around and around. He knew exactly how to suck it and lick it. Jamal got up and slid his long penis back into Alex, Jamal then lifted Alex's legs and began to slow stroke her gently. He wanted to feel all of her insides, Alex was wet and her clit gripped so tight on his penis.

"Baby, go harder," says Alex. Jamal lowered Alex's legs and turned her around. He then bent Alex over and started to pound his penis into her. All you heard was Alex's ass slapping against Jamal's tousle. After forty-five minutes of their sexual encounter, Jamal pulled out of Alex and nutted in his hand. They both slid to the floor to catch their breathe. Jamal rinsed his hands off.

He clapped twice, and the shower turned off. He knew how her body looked inside clothes, but without clothes he wanted her even more. Jamal knew Alex was the one; he felt their souls connect. All Alex could do was moan and call Jamal's name.

"Baby, that was amazing," says Alex. Jamal looked at Alex.

"Yes, it was," says Jamal. They both almost forgot they were even in the shower. They got out the shower grabbed towels and headed in the room for round two. Maya Angelo once said life is not measured by the number of breaths we take, but by the moments that take our breath away.

Chapter 6

Coby

*"Never make someone a priority when all you are to them
is an option."*
—*Maya Angelou*

"Rise and shine, my queen," says Jamal in that deep, sexy voice of his. Jamal had stared at Alex before he woke her up. Jamal reached over to kiss Alex in her sleep to wake her up. She rolled over and opened her eyes. Alex looked into Jamal's pretty eyes and just smiled.

"What time is it" says Alex?

"It is 9 a.m. baby. Breakfast will be ready in a minute. I hope you slept well," says Jamal.

Alex was a hard woman to please when it came to sex, but Jamal did his thing every time. Alex had spent the night with Jamal a couple of nights. This was the first time she had reached her sexual peak, and she kept coming back for more. Alex slept so well with all the kinks out of her body now.

Ladies, remember this, you can always write off a couple of sex partners and no one can judge you just let you know. You know what I mean, when you get the best sex in a long time your body feels different. What is the saying? It hits different when it's right.

The built-up pressure that Alex had from not having sex was worth it. If Jamal had popped the question right away, then maybe she would have said yes. She thought: *That was a joke; calm down.*

Jamal came through on his end and did not disappoint her by any means. Alex wanted to text the girls, but it would be obvious to Jamal. She could not even find her phone or her clothes. "Yes, I slept well, sweetie, thank you. But, where are my clothes?" says Alex.

"Baby that was the best sleep I got in a long time. I had Marta take them to get cleaned and steamed," says Jamal.

"You did not have to do that" says Alex. They were inter-rupted by the intercom.

"Mr. Stevenson breakfast is ready by the garden" says Marta over the loud speaker.

"Thank you, Marta, we will be down in a minute. Can you also bring Miss Douglas's clothes upstairs, please," says Jamal?

"Yes, sir" says Marta.

"Baby, are you ready to eat? I know you're hungry," says Jamal.

"You got jokes; I hope you are not throwing shade. I am hungry though," say Alex as she laughs.

"No, not at all; it's no shade. I want you to feed this fine-ass body of yours," says Jamal.

"Yea, I hear you, but I did burn calories, so I am starving," says Alex. Jamal gets up out of his bed and goes to the closet to get Alex a robe of his. Jamal puts on his robe. Jamal walks out the closet and back to the bed.

"Here is a robe for you, sweetheart, we are going to the garden," says Jamal. Alex pulls back the sheets and gets out of bed.

"You did not have to do all of that," says Alex. Jamal examines Alex's beautiful body once more in the light.

"Damn baby, why are you so perfect?" says Jamal.

"I'm far from perfect Jamal," says Alex.

Alex used to be body conscious back in the day. She has come a long way to feel confident about herself, so she knew her body was amazing. Alex put on the bath robe. They both walked out the room and headed to the elevator.

This house was amazing and stands alone, with a six-car garage. Jamal is only one person. It has seven bedrooms, and I know Marta stays in one. Jamal has an office and a gym, and eight bathrooms— how many toilets do you need? Alex thought.

Jamal had pictures of all of his family. Alex had learned that Jamal's grandmother raised him. His parents were both in the military. They were never around much. Jamal had so much respect for his grandmother, and she was his everything. Jamal had been a lawyer for ten years, and he had worked his way to the top. He was the best lawyer that his company had. Jamal had two sisters, and he was the oldest. When he got his first check, he brought it to his grandma, who he calls nana, for a franchise for the soul food restaurant. He respected her so much because she treated him and his sister like her own.

Jamal did not end up a statistic because his nana was on his ass. Jamal wanted to be a lawyer because he was in a program in high school that had them view different careers. Jamal made his extra money buying and flipping properties and also through the franchises. He and his nana owned four different restaurants in Boston. One of Jamal's sisters was a sports therapist, and the other was a cheerleader with the Boston Celtics.

Alex walked through the house and just imagined herself in the house, no harm in that. The house was laid out well, and Alex only wanted to see what else it had in it. Women are naturally nosey creatures; we want to know everything a man does not want us to know or tell us. If you say you are not nosey, you are a liar. We always want to know something that is not our business. Alex wanted to look in each room and look through all his stuff, but she knew she could not at this time. This house was decorated in some *Coming to America* style; there were so many antiques everywhere. Jamal was stacked, and this man was the man for Alex. Michelle was right about Jamal having moneyyyyy. Alex did not care about his money, though; he was different. Jamal gave her a feeling that a man has never given her before.

For instance, he had a real career, and it seemed as if his priorities were in the right place, not to mention he knew how to treat a real woman. Alex wanted love, loyalty, communication, commitment, and trustworthiness Jamal seemed to have it all. She was not rushing anything when it comes to relationships by any means, but she was interested to see where this went with Jamal. It is all in the timing—remember that, ladies. When both people come to the table, you both should have a full plate. Ladies, never mess with a man who has too much time on his hands; you will always run into problems. Have you ever heard the saying, mess with someone who is just as busy as you? Let that sizzle on your spirit. That statement is true because the ones who have time on their hands will constantly need something when you do not have time.

Alex and Jamal walked through the house to get to the garden. As they stepped into the garden, there were lights on the ground that came on. Jamal seemed to be a family man; he had a lot of pictures of his family and friends in the house. The breakfast spread had all type of options to choose from, like pancakes, waffles, French toast, fruit, coffee, tea, eggs, grits, salmon croquettes, potatoes, and much more. You would have thought he was feeding a small village. Alex almost called the girls to come by and get a plate. There was so much food. There was blue crystal and china that the food was placed on. It was amazing.

All Alex could think was *He took out the good dishes for me.* "Sweetheart, who are you trying to feed?" says Alex.

"All of the person in that robe of mine," says Jamal.

"Oh, so you have jokes?" says Alex. Alex left her phone in Jamal's bedroom, and she needed to check it asap.

"I will be back. I need to go and get my phone from your room to check on my daughter," says Alex.

"Sit down and relax. Marta can get it for you," says Jamal.

"No, she does not have to do that Jamal, I have two legs. I can get it," says Alex.

"That's what I pay her for," says Jamal. Alex looked at Jamal.

"Marta, can you get Miss Douglas's phone from the master suite?" says Jamal.

"How old is your daughter?" says Jamal.

"She is ten years old," says Alex. Alex felt like it was time for Leah Beloved to meet Jamal. She had been dating him for months, but things were good. Ladies, listen, no one can tell you who to bring around your child or children, but if it is right, go for it. Be honest with them. Jamal and Alex had been dating for months, and she had no ill feelings about him or his intentions. Marta returned to the garden and handed Alex her phone.

"Thank you, Marta," says Alex. "You're welcome, ma'am. Is there anything else I can do for you?" says Marta. Alex grabbed her phone and saw so many texts and missed calls.

"No, thank you, Marta. There is enough out here for you to grab a plate," says Alex.

"I am okay, ma'am," says Marta. Alex called her mom, but there was no answer. She called again and still no answer. Alex picked up her fork to eat her eggs and French toast. Alex called her house, and Stella answered the phone. "Hello, Douglas residence, how can I help you?" says Stella.

"Hi Stella, where is my mother?" says Alex.

"Hi, Miss Douglas, I am not sure. She left earlier," says Stella.

"Where is Leah Beloved," says Alex?

"She is in her room, Miss Douglas," says Stella.

"Let me speak to her," says Alex. Jamal sat across from Alex, and he just observed her. He loved how Alex was and how she demanded respect. Jamal knew Alex was a special woman. He did not try to listen to her conversation, but she was right across from him.

"Are you okay?" says Alex.

"Mom, yes, why wouldn't I be?" asked Leah.

"I am just asking. Leah Beloved. You usually call me. Where is your grandma? She called me seven times; is she okay?" says Alex.

"She wanted to know if I could go with her, but you never answered the phone," says Leah.

"Go where? You could have gone," says Alex.

"To Auntie Selene's house," says Leah Beloved.

"You could have gone with her your grandma, baby. She is so dramatic. Did you finish your homework?" says Alex.

"Mom it is the weekend," says Leah Beloved.

"Leah, I understand it is the weekend, but the quicker you get it done then the weekend is yours," says Alex.

"Yes, Mommy, I will get it done today," says Leah.

"Thank you and I love you. I will see you soon," says Alex.

"Love you too, Mommy," said Leah Beloved.

"Let me speak to Stella" says Alex.

"Yes, Mommy, and I love you too. Okay," says Leah.

"Hello, Mrs. Douglas," says Stella.

"Make sure she does that homework, and I will be home soon," says Alex.

"Yes, ma'am," says Stella.

"I will see you all in an hour or so," says Alex.

"Okay," says Stella. Alex hangs up the phone. Alex looks at her phone because the group chat was going ham; it was jumping like Jordan. Alex text the girls to tell them that she was okay and how things were going.

"Is everything okay, sweetie?" says Jamal.

"Yes, just needed to check on my baby and answer some emails from work," says Alex. Alex could not tell Jamal that she was texting her friends because you are never supposed to kiss and tell. But she had to because the "D" was just that good. She had to give her friends the 411. Now, ladies, only feed your friends a little information; there is no need to go all into details. That's just nasty.

Alex was being wined and dined like never before. Who was she kidding? She thought she was in a dream and needed to be pinched asap.

"I like how you handle your daughter," says Jamal.

"I have to stay on her to be great," says Alex. Jamal laughed and shook his head.

"It is the weekend, though, baby. Give her some freedom," says Jamal.

"I take education very seriously, that's all," says Alex.

"Baby, I see that. Calm down—I was just making a statement," says Jamal.

"I am calm, baby. I just take parenting seriously, and I did not mean to come at you like that," says Alex.

"Let's take her to the fair tonight," says Jamal.

"We can do that since you have not met her yet. That would be interesting," says Alex as she laughs. The two of them ate their breakfast and glanced at each other as they both ate. They gave each other the sex eyes as they ate breakfast and were undressing each other with their eyes. Alex's phone was blowing up with work emails, phone calls, and text messages. Alex did not want her time with Jamal to end, but it had to. Alex's phone rang again and again once more.

"Baby, you are popular," says Jamal.

"What can I say? I am a hot commodity," says Alex as she laughs. Alex answered the phone, and speak of the devil, look who it was—the devil himself. Coby started every conversation off as rude as all get out.

"Where is my baby?" saying Coby.

"My daughter is home where she needs to be." said Alex. Alex gets up from the table, she lips to Jamal, saying, *I'll be right back.* Jamal nods his head and watches Alex walk away.

"Why do you play these games with me?" says Coby.

"No one is playing with you; she is safe, so how can I help you?" says Alex.

"How can you help me? You must be around someone because you are showing off. Here you go with the goofy shit," says Coby.

"Why does that matter? I am busy, so I will call you back," says Alex.

"Alex, do not hang up this phone. We need to talk," say Coby as he raises his voice.

"Coby, I will not argue with you, especially when you pulled that shit in front of my office the other day," says Alex.

"You were not answering me," says Coby. Jamal was looking at Alex because her body language was off. He did not know what was going on.

"Coby, I will call you later," says Alex. Alex hung up the phone with Coby and looked at Jamal.

"Sorry about that," says Alex.

"Sweetheart, is everything okay?" says Jamal.

"Yes, love," says Alex. Alex was a woman who felt as if she did not have to explain herself to anyone or situations. She did not want to bring Jamal into the mix just yet. Alex did not want to lose what she has with Jamal because of Coby's stupid ass.

"Alex, do not lie to me," says Jamal.

"I know you heard that," says Alex.

"I was not in your conversation; I mind my business, love," says Jamal.

"Okay, but that is my daughter's father. He is the same guy who was outside my job the other day," says Alex.

"Since we are on the subject, what is the deal with that and him?" says Jamal. Alex hated being put on front street, but she needed to tell Jamal the tea of this relationship with her and Coby. In this time with Jamal, he had her nose wide open, so here goes nothing.

"Coby is Leah Beloved's father, he comes in and out of her life when he pleases. Coby is a big drug dealer here in Boston and other places. I keep my daughter away from the foolishness that he has going on," says Alex.

"So that is all?" says Jamal.

"What do you mean, is that all?" says Alex.

"He is the father of your child. Is anything else going on with you two?" says Jamal.

"No, we barely talk unless he is in town," says Alex.

"I believe you, baby. How long do I have you today?" says Jamal.

You have me for another hour or two hours" says Alex.

"Alex, I see the bond that we are building and he will not come in between that unless you let him" says Jamal. The magical words a woman wants to hear. Alex got up and went over to Jamal to sit in his lap.

"Are you done eating" says Jamal?

"Almost, why do you ask? I will not let him come in between this," said Alex. Jamal smiled and looked into Alex's eyes.

"I need some of that blackberry juice before you go," says Jamal.

"Blackberry juice?" says Alex.

Jamal looked at Alex and said, "I want you, baby." Alex knew she wanted him to tap her again. The thing was, could she take it? Jamal was hung like a horse, and she wanted every inch.

"You want to go back upstairs?" says Alex

"Why do we have to go upstairs?" says Jamal.

"What do you have in mind?" says Alex.

"You pick, sweetie; the house is mine" says Jamal. Alex forgot about finishing her breakfast, she stood up and opened her robe. The garden was beautiful, with roses, tulips, sunflowers, and other exotic flowers that looked expensive.

"Right here," says Jamal. Alex was all for it.

"I'm ready," says Alex. Jamal laughed as he got up from the table to grab Alex. Alex and Jamal walked over to the canopy in the yard. Alex's phone went off.

"You want to get that, baby," says Jamal.

"No, they can wait," says Alex. Alex and Jamal start to kiss, she is on top of him. Alex phone goes off again. They both ignore it and keep kissing. Jamal lifts Alex up slightly and stick his long penis into her. Alex tilts her head back and moans. Jamal bounces Alex up and down on his penis. Alex's head goes back as she is basking in the moment with Jamal.

Alex phone goes off again. Forty-five minutes go by and they are both drenched in sweat. "Damn baby" says Jamal. "What baby" says Alex as she is slow grinding on Jamal? "You are amazing" says Jamal. "No, you are amazing" says Alex. Alex moaned and grabbed Jamal's shoulders. Jamal grabbed Alex's ass, kept digging his penis into her. Alex nuts and falls to the side of Jamal. Alex takes the robe and covers herself. "Sweetheart, I need to take a shower" says Alex. "Baby go ahead" says Jamal. "You cannot keep doing that to me" says Alex. Alex grabs her phone to see fifteen text messages from Coby, threatening her. She knew just how to handle Coby, and she was going to do just that.

"I am giving you everything you deserve," says Jamal. Alex kissed Jamal once more and went to take a shower.

Chapter 7

Drastic Times Call for Drastic Measures

"As one goes through life one learns that if you don't paddle your own canoe, you don't move."
—Katharine Hepburn

Like I said before, ladies, please let these men know who you are. At times, you have to put your foot down. Yes, you can let a man be a man, but you need to demand respect. Some men get besides themselves. You as a woman sometimes have to bring them back to reality from time to time. Now I'm not saying put your hands on anyone unless it is self-defense. A real woman can demand respect without violence.

"Hello," says Coby.

"Meet me at Junior's now," says Alex. Alex hung up and headed to the hole in the wall called Junior's. Junior's was a place that Alex and Coby used to go; it was a little hole in the wall that had the best philly cheesesteaks ever. When Coby took Alex on their first date, they came to this place. This was back when she was a struggling student, and he was just a corner boy. They were both pushing pennies and broke, but they made it in their own ways. Alex drove to Junior's thinking about what she was going to say to Coby. She didn't want to curse at him or start a confrontation with him. She just wanted to get her point across and make him understand her position. Coby knows how to bring that side out of Alex, and she was tired of it. Alex hated getting out of character for anyone, including her no-good baby daddy. She didn't even like using the word *baby daddy* because it was so ghetto.

Alex's car phone is going off.

"Hello," says Alex.

"Hey, my beautiful queen," says Jamal.

"Hey, handsome" says Alex as she has this big smile on her face.

"Oh, handsome huh?" says Jamal.

"Yes, love," says Alex.

"What are you up to, baby?" says Jamal.

"I am about to handle some business," says Alex.

"You sound like you mean business," says Jamal.

"I do mean business. What's my name?" says Alex.

"Alex," says Jamal in a deep sexy voice. When he said it, he made Alex's panties wet. Alex laughed at Jamal. Alex is pulling up to Junior's and sees Coby sitting in the window. Mind you, Coby is never on time to nothing.

"Baby, I will call you back in a minute. I need to walk into this building," says Alex.

"Do I need to beat up anyone?" says Jamal.

"No, I will handle it," says Alex.

"Okay, sweetheart. You know I am on standby," says Jamal. Alex hangs up the phone and steps out of the car. She clicks the button to her car and walks into Junior's. She already saw Coby and walked over to the table he was sitting at.

"Hello, Alex," says Coby. Alex puts her hand up to cut him off and sits down. Coby was about to start talking. Alex cut him off and went in.

"Let me tell you something, the next time you think you can threaten me. You better come through with it. I was trying to be nice and not do this to you, but you have pushed me to the edge. From showing up to my job, to the twenty-something text messages I cannot deal. I do not want something happening to my daughter because of your enemies. That is why I keep you away, if you want the truth, Coby. I am not one of those hood-rat chicks you deal with. You have tried it and pushed things too far. You cannot just pop in and pop out of her life like popcorn. She needs stability, which she has with me. Her schedule does not need to be broken because sometimes you want to play daddy. You give her broken promises all the time, and it hurts her. Guess who has to be there picking up the pieces? I'm the only one wiping tears, not you. I am not even the same girl I used to be. I grew up, and you need to do the same if you want to be a part of her daughter's life. You cannot see Leah Beloved, and if you come anywhere near me or her again, I will destroy you, and that is not a threat. It's a promise" says Alex.

"Alex, I'm sorry. I wanted to get your attention," says Coby.

"You're right; you are sorry. I never asked you for shit, nor did I look for you to do anything for Leah Beloved," says Alex.

"I want you to, though. I know you have been doing things alone," says Coby.

"I cannot take blood money from you," says Alex.

"It is not bloody money. I have investments," says Coby.

"Coby, I do not have time for your bullshit," says Alex.

"I do not want to hold you up," says Coby. Yes, Alex was being hard on him, but she was over the bullshit with him. Alex was frustrated because he was doing way too much. She wanted her life to go back to normal.

"I do not even need money from you, I need you to be a father to her" says Alex.

"Can we come to an agreement?" says Coby

"An agreement?" says Alex with a puzzled look on her face.

"Yes, an agreement for me to see Leah," says Coby.

"I will think about it," says Alex. Alex gets up to leave the restaurant.

"Wait," says Coby.

"What, Coby," says Alex.

"Can you at least think about it?" says Coby. Alex looks at him and walks to the exit.

"I will consider it." says Alex.

She looks back at Coby one more time and walks to her car. Alex gets in the car and starts to cry. She hated to be mean, but she had to give tough love. It is not that Alex is bitter or nasty. Alex is protecting her daughter from the drug life that Coby lived. Alex had been a single parent for ten years, and it was her job to keep her daughter's best interests at heart. When a man is living that life, they always have enemies. These people are not just killing you, they are killing your family as well. It is a dirty, dirty world that we live in. Alex knew that she had to keep her daughter safe by any means necessary.

Alex knew the only person that would understand is Michelle, so she picked up the phone and called her. Alex was still weeping but pulled herself together. As she pulled off the road, Michelle picked up the phone.

"What's wrong, Alex? Are you crying?" says Michelle.

"I was. I just left after talking to Coby," says Alex.

"Lord what happened, and where are you? Do I need to put on my sneakers," says Michelle.

"No, I need to talk to you. Where are you?" says Alex.

"I'm at the shop, balancing the books. Come by," says Michelle.

"I'm on the way," says Alex.

"Okay, be safe" says Michelle. Alex hangs up and headed towards the shop.

You always have to have your good girlfriends about certain situations. But in the meantime, make sure you have to go to that friend who has common sense as well. For example, you have that one friend who does not have a man. You have man problems, and she is going to tell you drop his ass and let's hang out and be a hoe together. That friend just wants someone else with her while she is tricking; she cannot relate because she has no man. Alex is not going to go to Honestie or Camilla because neither one of them have children.

Neither of them knows what it feels like to be a single parent, either. So, you cannot expect them to understand or look to have your child's best interest at heart at a time like this. Michelle understands what Alex is going through because Michelle's husband is incarcerated, and she is technically a single parent right now until he returns. Also, her husband was in the drug game. Their daughters were the same age, so it was perfect. She would know how to go about this situation in the right way without all the extra shit. Alex needs help and was not afraid to ask for it. Alex pulled up to the shop, got out the car, and knocked on the door of the shop.

Michelle was there waiting at the door with a glass of wine. "Come on; let's talk," says Michelle. Alex and Michelle head over to the waiting area to sit on the big fluffy couch that made her ass feel good.

"I told you I was with Coby," says Alex.

"Yes, you did. So, what happened?" says Michelle.

"We had a conversation about Leah Beloved. He wants to see her, but I told him I would think about it," says Alex.

"What do you mean he wants to see her?" says Michelle.

"He wants to be in her life, and all this other stuff," says Alex.

"Alex to be honest, I love you, but I am going to tell you the true tea, no sugar-coating things. You are kind of stuck between a rock and a hard place. Leah is at an age where she understands, so you need to sit down and talk to her," says Michelle.

"I am not bringing my daughter into this foolishness," says Alex.

"You have to, boo; it is her right to choose, and it is her father," says Michelle.

Alex started to cry again because for a long time, Alex kept Leah Beloved out of that life. It was easy for her not to talk about Coby because he was not around.

"Stop crying Alex, you are the strongest woman I know. You're not bringing her into this life, you are letting her father in. When my husband was sent to prison, it was the hardest thing for me and my baby. We as her parents had to come to a common ground to say if she was going to go to the prison to see her father," says Michelle.

"I understand everything that you are saying; I just want her to be okay," says Alex.

"Alex do you really think her father will not harm her," says Michelle?

"Yes, I do. I need to talk to Leah Beloved, but it is my job to keep my child safe," says Alex.

"I get that, Alex, but let her make her own decisions about her father," says Michelle.

We as women tend to convince ourselves that something is right when it is not always right. Deep down, we know we are wrong, but for us to sleep at night we make up these lies in our heads or overthink things. Whether you feel like Alex is wrong or right, it is something for you to think about. Before you can judge the next person, put yourself in that person's shoes.

"Thank you for being my friend," says Alex.

"You know I am here for you," says Michelle.

"I know. Let me get home to Leah Beloved so we can talk," says Alex. "I haven't been home all day."

"Where have you been?" says Michelle. Alex looks at Michelle and sticks her tongue out.

"I was with Jamal again," says Alex.

"Really? It is getting serious," says Michelle.

"Yes, it is, but I will tell you more at a later date," says Alex.

"Trust me, I completely understand," says Michelle. Alex and Michelle finish sipping their wine, and Alex leaves the shop to go home. Alex thinks about what Michelle says on the way home. Alex pulls up to her house and sits there. She did not want to face Leah Beloved, but she knew she had to. Alex got out the car, and she walked into her house. When she walked in the house, she puts her keys in the bowl and takes off her shoes at the door.

"Hello, Miss Douglas," says Stella.

"Hello, Stella, you can go home. Thank you so much," says Alex.

"Have a great afternoon," says Stella.

"Okay, you as well. Oh, where is Leah Beloved?" saying Alex.

"She is in the living room," says Stella.

"Thank you, Stella, for today," says Alex.

"Yes, ma'am, Miss Douglas, have a nice night," says Stella. Stella grabs her purse and coat. She goes to the door and lets herself out.

"Leah Beloved," says Alex.

"Yes, Mommy," says Leah Beloved. Alex walks through the long hallway to get to the living room. Leah was sitting on the turquoise couch, watching her favorite movie. She turned around and looked at Alex. Alex looked at Leah Beloved, took a deep breath, and walked toward her. Alex sat on the couch next to Leah Beloved.

"Hey, Mommy, how was your day?" says Leah.

"It was good, baby, and yours?" says Alex. "Did you do your homework?"

"Yes, Mom," says Leah Beloved. Leah was texting Michelle's daughter.

"Leah, put your phone down. We need to talk," says Alex.

"What did I do?" says Leah.

"Nothing, baby; just listens to me," says Alex.

"Yes, ma'am," says Leah. Alex scooted closer to Leah.

"I saw your father today, and I think you are old enough to understand what is going on," says Alex.

"Okay," says Leah.

"I have told your father that he cannot see you, but I want you to make that decision," says Alex.

"Why is that?" saying Leah.

"Your father is into some things that I personally do not think that you should be around, but it is your decision if you want him to be in your life," says Alex.

"Mom, I love my dad, and even though he is not always around, I do want to see him," says Leah Beloved.

"I just want to protect you," says Alex.

"I know, Mom, but it will always be me and you," say Leah Beloved. Alex looked at her daughter, and all she could do was cry. Her baby was growing up right before her eyes, and she was so proud.

"Okay will I will text you his number, and you can call him," says Alex.

"Okay, Mom. Do not cry; everything will be fine," says Leah Beloved.

Alex wiped her face and hugged Leah.

"Okay, what are you watching?" says Alex.

"That movie I was watching with Grandma, *Stir Crazy*," says Leah Beloved.

"You have watched this movie a million times," says Alex.

"It is funny, Mom," says Leah Beloved as she laughs.

"Well, I'm going to watch it with you. Do you want ice cream, boo?" says Alex.

"Yes, Mom, thanks" say Leah Beloved. Alex got off the couch to walk to the kitchen.

Women talk to your children; they understand more than you think. Keep it real with them. You do not always have to baby your children.

Chapter 8

Destruction at Its Finest

"The final forming of a person's character lies in their hands."
—Anne Frank

When life seems as if it is going well, there is always something that goes wrong. The devil is always busy, remember that. It is like when you go through a break up. Once you break up with that individual who was not good for you, good things start to happen for you. For instance, your edges start to grow back, your credit score goes up 200 points, you lose that small pudge you have been trying to get rid of for a couple of months, people see a glow on you, and all your bills get caught up and paid. Oh, and not to mention, you may be getting that promotion you have been waiting on. Ladies, it is called drop-dead weight, stop holding on to relationships and friendships that do not mean a thing to you.

The girls always met at least once a week at least to catch up and spill the tea. You always need to spill tea with your good girlfriends every now and again. Let me tell you what's going on because this kettle was hot honey; the water is boiling on this good stove, and all the teas needed to be aired out. "Pressed,

Pressed, Pressed" by Cardi B was playing on low in the background while the girls were at Alex's house.

"I brought the Moet" says Honestie. Alex grabs wine glasses out of the kitchen.

"Where is late ass Camilla," says Michelle.

"She is on her way," says Alex as she laughs.

"Where is Leah?" says Michelle? Alex rolls her eyes.

"She is with her father," says Alex.

"Her father?" both girls said at the same time.

"Michelle, do not do that. You told me to do it," says Alex.

"*No, no, no*; I said talk to her to see where her head was at," says Michelle.

"Whatever, Michelle," says Alex.

I know what you are thinking: how could Alex let Leah go with her father? That is just it; the key word is *father*. Ladies, sometimes you have to let that individual I really want to call the N word hang themselves. Let your child make the decision because you will only hurt them in the end. I know some of you are rolling your eyes, but hear me out on this: a wise person once told me, "Do not block your blessings being nasty."

"So, what is new ladies?" says Honestie. They heard a knock at the door.

"That must be Camilla," says Alex. Camilla comes through the door.

"Heyyyyyy, girls, do I have some stuff to tell y'all," says Camilla.

"So do I," says Alex.

"I know y'all are always waiting on me, sorry," says Camilla.

"You're always sorry," says Michelle as she laughs.

"Alex, how is that fine-ass Jamal?" says Honestie.

"He is amazing. He and Leah Beloved are getting to know each other," says Alex.

"Yassss, I am so happy you let your guard down. Did you say Leah and he are getting to know each other?" says Camilla.

"Yes, he has met her, and we have gone on dates, done dinner, and he has even spent the night here," says Alex.

"There is a glow all around you. I am so happy for you, boo," says Michelle.

"Y'all stop it, but he did this to me. There is just something about him that I cannot put my finger on," says Alex.

"I am surprised that you let him meet Leah," says Honestie. Alex smiles because she is finally happy.

"Girls, so it's my turn. I met this guy at the coffee shop on last week, he is so fine, and we have been on two dates so far," says Camilla.

"Wait one minute, two dates?" says Alex.

"You heffa—you've been keeping secrets," says Honestie.

"No, I'm not but y'all know how I am," says Camilla.

"What does that heffa say?" says Alex as she sips her wine.

"Look to my defense, I have not had sex with him," says Camilla.

"Now this is a record for you, hun," says Honestie.

"You know my motto; I have to see what you are working with before I am all in. Also, I am sensing major shade," says Camilla.

"That is a bad motto," says Michelle as she laughs. Time was going by, and the girls were on bottle number two of their wine. They laughed, joked around, and talked for hours.

The girls were gathered in Alex's living room.

"Who wants Chinese? I'm hungry," says Michelle.

"The menu is in the third drawer," says Alex. Everyone knew in Boston that Mr. Chan's was the late-night spot for fresh Chinese food that was the best. Michelle was looking through the drawers.

"Found it," says Michelle.

"I want the shrimp low mein," says Honestie.

"Sesame chicken and cream cheese wontons for me," says Camilla.

"Fried chicken and shrimp fried rice for me," says Alex.

Alex's phone rung. "Hello," says Alex. Alex got up and stepped out of the room. It was Coby on the phone, but nothing was said. "Hello, Hello, hello," says Alex. Alex hung up the phone and walked back in the living room. The girl placed their orders with Michelle while she talked to the owner on the phone.

"Alex, is Leah spending the night with Coby?" says Michelle.

"Hell, no; she is coming home. Damn, it is late. He just called but said nothing on the phone," said Alex.

"Well, call her," says Michelle as she hangs up the phone with the Chinese restaurant. Alex is not trying to show panic, but she is panicking inside; the girls were right. It was late, and she had not heard from Leah; her stomach was in knots.

"I'm going to just check on her. I have that right," says Alex. Alex calls Leah, no answer. Alex calls Leah again, still no answer. Alex pulls up Leah's phone from hers, to look up her location and she sees that she is at a standstill on 114th street and Myers. Alex calls Coby, and there is no answer.

"Neither one of them is answering the phone," says Alex.

"Do not panic," says Michelle.

"How the hell can I not panic? It says they are on 114th street," says Alex.

"Why would they be there?" says Honestie? Alex picks up her phone and paces back and forth. She calls Leah's phone again, still no answer.

"There are a bunch of warehouses on 114th Street. I sold one to a client," says Camilla.

"Come on, let's get into the car and go over there," says Michelle.

"We have been drinking. I'll call my driver," says Alex.

They heard a knock at the front door of Alex's house.

"Damn, that can't be the food already. I'll get it" says Camilla. Camilla gets off the couch and walks toward the door and opens it as Alex is trying to call Leah again.

"How can I help you?" says Camilla as she stares at the man in the doorway. Alex, Michelle. and Honestie look toward the door.

"Can I come in?" says the man.

"How can I help you first sir? You can not just come in here," says Camilla?

"Hello, is Miss Douglas here?" says the man at the door. Alex walks to the door to see what his man wanted and to see who he could be.

"Umm, hello, I am Miss Douglas; how can I help you?" says Alex. The girls are looking at the man. making sure that everything was okay with Alex.

"I am Detective Martins," says the man.

"Okay, now once again how can I help you—wait did you say Detective?" says Alex.

Camilla stands next to Alex and looks the detective up and down. He is fine and packing, the gun she means, as Camilla thought in her head.

"Is your daughter's name Leah Beloved Douglas?" saying Detective Martins.

"Yes, it is. What is going on? Is she okay?" says Alex. Michelle and Honestie were standing behind Alex. Alex is shaking, not knowing what this man is about to tell her.

"There was a shootout on 114th street at 8:00 p.m. She and her father were in the middle of it. Your daughter is at the hospital with multiple gunshot wounds," says Detective Martins.

"The hospital—is my baby okay?" says Alex as she grabs her stomach and starts to cry. Alex lost her balance and stumbled. Alex almost fell, but Michelle broke her fall. The detective continues to talk, but Alex can barely hear anything. She was blacking out.

"Your daughter was shot three times, and her father is with her at the hospital," says Detective Martins. Alex gathers herself and looks at the detective.

"Which hospital are they going to?" says Alex as she cries.

"They are at Shriners Hospitals for Children," says Detective Martins."

"Grab my phone and purse," says Alex as she screams at the girls. Alex grabs her keys off the keyring by the door and pushes past the detective to run out the door.

"Miss Douglas, I still have questions to ask you," says Detective Martins as he yells to Alex. Alex continues to run to her car parked in the front of the driveway. Alex hops in her car and sped off, not looking behind her. Michelle, Camilla, and Honestie hop in Michelle's car, leaving the officer at the door.

"Sir, meet us at the hospital," says Michelle. Detective Martins closes Alex's front door and walks to his cruiser. They followed behind her. Alex is speeding to the hospital, going a hundred miles per hour. She could care less about traffic; she had tunnel vision. Alex had to get to her baby. She cannot think of anything but if Leah Beloved was alone or if she was scared. All these thoughts were running through Alex mind at one time. *How did this happen? Where were they? Who shot her baby?* Alex runs the light and turns the corner. She finally pulls up to the hospital. She hops out her car in the emergency line and runs to the front desk. Alex car was still running.

"Excuse me, excuse me, my daughter was shot. Her name is Leah Beloved Douglas. Where is she?" said Alex franticly as she is pacing back and forth at the nurse's station.

"Ma'am, I need you to calm down," says the nurse.

"I will not calm down. She is a minor. I need to know what is going on," says Alex as she continues to yell. Alex at this point is blaming herself because she should have never let Leah Beloved go with Coby. Alex wouldn't know what to do if she lost Leah. Alex could not stop crying because no one was saying anything.

"Let me get the doctor," says the nurse. The nurse gets up from the station and walks down the hallway to see if the doctor was available. Camilla and Honestie came up behind Alex.

"What is going on?" they both say.

"I do not know, the nurse went to get the doctor. She will not say anything," says Alex.

"Michelle is parking your car," says Camilla. Alex looks up and spots Coby coming down the hall with a patch on his head, a sling on his arm, and blood on his clothes. Coby had his head in his hands, knowing he had messed up. He was crying. Alex only had rage in her eyes. Alex runs over to him because she wanted to know what happened.

"What happened to my damn child?" says Alex yelling and pointing in his face.

"Get out my face, Alex. She is my child as well" says Coby calmly as he stares at Alex. He could see the hurt in her eyes. Michelle walks into the emergency room. He did not know how to answer her or what to say. Alex slaps Coby in the face out of nowhere.

"I trusted you with *my* daughter, and this shit happens. You have nothing to say?" says Alex.

Women tend to throw around the *my* word a lot when you are the primary parent. It gives you a sense of entitlement. Honestly, when you are the primary parent, you can use that word. Alex hits Coby again.

Coby is now in Alex's face, and he goes to raise his hand at Alex when Camilla, Honestie, and Michelle say at the same time, "I wish you would just stop."

Yes, Alex was mad, and she should not have been putting her hands on Coby, but she needed answers, and he was not cooperating. Michelle pulls Alex back from Coby. Everyone was staring at them. Security started to walk over to try to defuse the situation.

"You had one job," says Alex as she yells at Coby because Michelle was still holding her back. With all the drama going on, no one noticed the doctor coming around the corner.

"Are you Miss Douglas? I am Doctor Richards," saying the doctor. Alex breaks away from Michelle.

"Yes, that is me," says Alex.

"You're the parent of Leah Beloved Douglas?" says Doctor Richards.

"Yes, I am. What is going on with my baby?" says Alex, trying to get the information out of the doctor. The doctor starts to speak about Leah Beloved. Alex falls to the ground as he is talking; she could not believe what was happening.

"She was shot three times, once in the leg, her side, and her arm. She is stable for now, but one of the bullets hit her large intestine. She lost a lot of blood, so we have to wait to do the rest of the surgery," says Doctor Richards. Camilla is holding Alex as she cries aloud.

"When can we see here?" says Michelle.

"We are doing what we can; the bullets in her arm and leg are out. The one in her side is tricky and if it is not taken out right, things could go badly," says Doctor Richards.

"Can I see her?" says Alex.

"Give us some time to get her stabilized, and I will come get you. For now, have a seat in the lobby, and we will keep you posted," says Doctor Richards.

"I need her to know that I am here," says Alex. The girls tried to keep Alex calm.

"I will let you know when you can go in, Miss Douglas," says Doctor Richards. Doctor Richards turned to go back down the hall.

Alex was all over the place. She walked to the lobby and sat where she could see the hallway.

"Who has my phone? I need to call my mom, my sisters, my boss, and her school," says Alex. She was scrambling to look for her phone. Alex is talking so fast that the girls are trying to keep up with what she was saying.

"I'll call your mom," says Camilla.

"I will call your sisters; just sit down and be still, Alex," says Michelle.

"Alex, you have to calm down for Leah. When you see her you need to be at your best," says Camilla. Honestie looked at Alex's phone, and Jamal had called twice, so Honestie called him.

"I cannot sit down; my child is in there fighting for her life," says Alex as she paced back and forth in the lobby, waiting for the doctor to come back out.

The lobby was loud, and so much was going on. The phone was ringing, the nurses were calling patients, and the ambulance was bringing someone else in.

"Have you called Jamal?" says Michelle. Alex did not answer her; she would not even look up at anyone. All the girls were on the phone making the necessary calls for Alex.

"Your mom is flying in tomorrow," says Camilla.

"Your sisters are on the way," says Michelle. Honestie was on the phone with Jamal.

"Hello, beautiful," says Jamal.

"This is not Alex, this is Honestie, her best friend. She cannot talk right now" says Honestie.

"Why can she not talk? What is wrong with her?" says Jamal. Jamal was raising his voice a little.

"Hey, calm down, hun. Her daughter was shot, and we are at the hospital now," says Honestie.

"Leah was shot? How? What happened?" says Jamal.

"We do not know the full story yet," says Honestie.

"I am on the way; which hospital are y'all at?" says Jamal.

"We are at Shriners Hospital," says Honestie.

"Okay, I am going to be there in ten minutes," says Jamal. Honestie could hear Jamal shuffling in the background.

"We are in the lobby," says Honestie. Jamal and Honestie hung up the phone.

"Alex, Jamal is on his way," says Honestie. Alex looked up and eyed Coby as they sat in the waiting room. Coby was across the room waiting to see what the doctor was going to say. Alex wanted to beat his ass, but what would it solve. Alex thought to herself: *How much time would I get if I killed his ass? He does not even know what I am capable of at this point in my life. This is my fault. I should have told his ass no. I failed my daughter.* Alex just wanted Leah to be okay.

Chapter 9

Light at the End of the Tunnel

*"She was afraid of heights, but she was much more afraid
of Never flying."*
—Atticus

The sun was starting to peek through the window of the hospital lobby. Everyone was still waiting to hear what going on with Leah. The nurse came from behind the desk.

"Miss Douglas can you fill out this paperwork?" says the nurse. Alex grabbed the information and started to fill it out. Jamal was sitting next to Michelle, and Alex's sisters were sitting next to Honestie and Camilla. Alex could not sit down. She had a lot to get off her chest, but it was not the right time. She was still upset and scared all at the same time. Alex walked over to Coby.

"I am calling my lawyer today. You will never see my child again," says Alex.

"This is not my fault," says Coby.

"Never—how is it not your damn fault and my child is fighting for her life in that room? I am two seconds off your ass," says Alex as she screams at him. Coby could not do anything but shake his head. He was really not sure what happened.

"You think I want her to be in there and not me?" says Coby. Alex could not stop crying as she paced back and forth.

"I wish it was you in there than her," says Alex.

"Damn, Alex, that is how you feel?" says Coby.

"That is exactly how I feel. I wish you had died a long time ago," says Alex.

"What is going on?" says Brook as she came through the door.

"I do not know; he will not say shit," says Alex as she points to Coby sitting across the room with this stupid look on his face. Brook and Selene looked at Coby because neither one of them could stand him or even liked him before this. Selene was the sister that did not care what she said out of her mouth.

"Soooooo, you are not going to tell my sister what happened to her damn daughter? We have been here for hours," says Selene as she yells at Coby. I know what everyone is thinking, they are teaming up on Coby. But he had been quiet, processing this shit in his head.

"That is right, he was supposed to protect Leah. He made me a fucking a promise," says Alex. Alex sat next to Jamal. Camilla shook her head.

"Has the doctor come back out here?" says Brook.

"They had to stabilize her. She had lost a lot of blood and was shot in the leg and her side is all they said," says Alex.

"Where is Mom?" said Selene.

"I am not sure. I have not talked to her," says Alex.

"Did anyone call her," says Brook?

"Yes, I did," says Camilla.

Jamal looked at Alex. "Baby, can I get you some coffee?"

"No, baby, I am okay," says Alex.

"I'll be right back, love," says Jamal. Alex was coming down from her rage when Detective Martins walks in. Alex rolled her eyes as he walked over to her.

"Hello, Miss Douglas," says detective Martins.

"Unless you tell me what happened with my daughter because that idiot is not saying shit, you are dismissed," says Alex. When Alex said that, everyone looked at the detective to see his response. Alex was pissed, and at this point anyone could get it.

"That is what I am trying to find out for you," says Detective Martins. Detective Martins turned from Alex and walked over to Coby.

"Hello, Mr. Brooks, can you tell me what happened?" says Detective Martins.

"Hi sir," says Coby.

"We did not get a chance to talk at the crime scene," says Detective Martins.

"All I know, I was sitting at the light, and a black Tahoe with tinted windows pulled up and started shooting. I sped off, and they followed me down the alley," says Coby. Coby's phone was going off.

"You need to get that," says Detective Martins.

"No, I will call them back," says Coby. Coby knew what that call was, but he could not get it.

"Did you see anyone in the vehicle," says Detective Martins?

"No, I saw a mask peeking through the window," says Coby.

Alex was about to say something else when Jamal came around the corner.

"Hey, baby, what is going on?" says Jamal.

"His ass is talking to the police," says Alex.

"He is finally speaking?" saying Jamal.

"Her sperm donor has a voice now," says Alex. Coby gets up and walks past the detective. He walks toward Alex.

"You not going to keep disrespecting me," says Coby. Coby pointed his finger at Alex's face. Jamal jumped in front of Alex, and all the girls stood up.

"Now I will tell you this one time and one time only. If you ever walk up on my woman again, you will not walk again, player," says Jamal. Honestie, Camilla, and Michelle looked at each other and sat down. Jamal definitely had things handled.

"Who is this goofy ass nigga?" saying Coby.

"I'm your worst damn nightmare—now step off," says Jamal. Coby looked at Alex, then at Jamal, and walked toward the exit of the hospital.

"Mr. Brooks, we are not done yet," says Detective Martins. He follows Coby to the door.

"This not over, Alex. You will have to see me," says Coby. Coby leaves, and Alex looks in Jamal's eyes.

"Baby, I got you," says Jamal.

"Girl, we are here, we got you, too," says Michelle.

"Who is the doctor?" said Jamal.

"Doctor Richards or something like that," says Camilla.

"Doug Richards?" says Jamal.

"We are not sure," says Honestie.

"Let me go see," says Jamal.

Jamal gets up and goes to the nurse's station and talks to the nurse at the station.

"Hello, I need to find out if that is Doctor Doug Richards on my girlfriend's daughter's surgery," says Jamal.

"Sure, let me look," says the nurse as she batted her eyes at Jamal. You could tell the nurse was flirting with Jamal. Hell, whose panties would not get wet; he was fine as hell. The nurse looks at her computer and could barely speak when she looked at Jamal.

"Yes, sir it is. I am really not supposed to give that out," says the nurse.

"Thank you, sweetheart," says Jamal. Jamal turned to leave the nurses station when Doctor Richards came around the corner.

"Is that oddball Jamal?" says Doctor Richards.

"Yes, it is. How are you? Long time no see," says Jamal. Alex gets up and walks over to them talking.

"What are you doing here?" says Doctor Richards.

"My girlfriend's daughter was the one who was shot," says Jamal.

"Wow, this is a small world," says Doctor Richards.

"How is my daughter?" says Alex, interrupting the conversation.

"She is stable. We were able to remove the bullet in her side," says Doctor Richards.

"Thank you. When can I see her?" says Alex.

"We are taking her to a recovery room, and then you will be able to see her," says Doctor Richards.

"Take care of her daughter, man. We will catch up," says Jamal.

"I will, bro, nice seeing you. Mis. Douglas, can I talk to you please," says Doctor Richards. Alex was scared to know what he had to say.

"Yes, doctor," says Alex.

"I just want you to be prepared, but Leah Beloved may not walk again. The bullet was too close to her spine," says Doctor Richards.

"She what?" says Alex in a lifted voice. Alex was holding her stomach, with her hand on her mouth. Everyone turned around. Jamal walked over to Alex.

"Alex, what is wrong?" says Jamal.

In a whispering voice, Alex said, "Leah may not walk again." Jamal looked at Doctor Richards. Doctor Richards mouthed to Jamal, "I am sorry, bro." Then he walked away. Jamal held Alex in arms as she cried. She could not believe this news. Her baby may not walk again. Alex walked over to the chair she was sitting in. She looked at everyone.

"Leah may not walk again," says Alex. Everyone was quiet. It was so quiet you could hear a rat piss on cotton.

Camilla knew it was not the time, but she was going to ask Jamal about his friend when all was said and done. Camilla was always on the prowl.

"Damn," says Michelle. You could see the tears rolling down her face.

"Thank you for being here, but you all can go home. They are putting her in recovery, and then I will be able to see her," says Alex. The crew was tired; they had been there for hours.

"Alex, I will go check on your house and let Stella know what's going on," says Honestie.

Alex's sisters got up and kissed her on her head. Everyone got up to leave. Alex sat in the lobby on pause. She was in a daze. When she came back from outer space, she looked at Jamal.

"You can go home. I am glad you came," says Alex.

"Yes, I did come, baby. That's your child in there, and if we date, she matters to me also," says Jamal. Alex was vulnerable, and Jamal was saying a lot of things that she wanted to hear. He was right, but in her eyes, they were boyfriend and girlfriend. Hell, she was not letting him go after how he showed out the other night and stood up for her with Coby. There is a saying, "You fuck with me, you stuck with me." Alex was loyal to those who were loyal to her. Jamal had more than proved himself to her. It had been six months. He was consistent and a man that she wanted around.

"Thank you, Jamal," says Alex.

"I want her to be okay because I cannot imagine what you are going through at this moment. I know she means the world to you," says Jamal. Alex looks at Jamal and continues to cry in his arms. She felt weak and helpless. At this point, her walls came all the way down because this man was what she had craved, and she knew he was by her side. Alex never felt so safe in this time of crisis.

Chapter 10

When You Know It's Right?

*"She was afraid of heights, but she was much more afraid
of Never flying."*
—Atticus

*I*t has been a month, and Leah was about to be released
from the hospital. Alex was sleeping at Leah's bedside in a
chair that was hurting her back. Alex switched positions in the
reclining chair.

"Ma'am, ma'am," says the nurse as she tapped Alex's leg. Alex
wakes up and looks at Leah and then at the nurse.

"Yes, how can I help you?" says Alex.

"Go home and get some rest. She will be fine," says the nurse.

"I am not leaving her; she is my baby," says Alex.

"I will stay in here with her while you go home and at least
shower. You have been here every day, all day," says the nurse.
Alex lifted her arms and made a weird face, she knew she was
funky, but the fact of her baby may be waking up and her not
being there scared her. Leah was still in a lot of pain, and there
was no way that she should wake up and her mom not be there.
The surgery went well, but the recovery time was going to be a

process. Alex knew what was up ahead for this journey. With all that had happened, Alex wanted to ensure that Leah was safe by any means necessary. She would not let anything happen to Leah again. Alex was going to square up with anyone if a hair was out of place on Leah Beloved's head.

Alex felt guilty and did not know how to shake the feeling. *Was it her fault?* No, it was not, but she continued to blame herself. Let me spill this tea because this kettle is hot. I know you were waiting on what happened. Coby is nowhere to be found, if you were wondering. He had not been back since Leah got out of surgery, and the police still have questions about that night. He is looking really suspect, if you ask me. He has not called or checked in since. Alex knew when she saw him, that she was going to ring his neck. She wanted him dead, and no one could change her mind about how she felt. She had to really pray to God for forgiveness. Alex could always call in a favor, but could she really live with herself? Jamal is still holding on, well holding her down in this time, I should say. Everyone had come through for Alex and was there for her. Alex had stayed by Leah Beloved's side this whole time. She barely left her side, and I mean barely; you hear me?

Alex was in her thoughts. *My baby is in this hospital bed, and all I can think about is taking away her pain.* Jamal was amazing, like her knight in shining armor. Alex could not even get through what she had going on without the support system. Jamal had run errands for her, brought her food, and made sure Leah Beloved was getting the best care. Not to mention, he had hired a private nurse to stay at the house for Leah when she gets released.

Alex is falling for Jamal day by day. She could not stop her feelings for him. He had made it so easy. She felt like he had built the wall of China with an electric fence and guard dogs around her. Alex has never felt like this before; this feeling was like a dream come true that she did not want to wake up from. Yes, she had had other relationships, but no one cared as much or even cared about her as a person. So now you are caught up on what is going on.

"Okay, okay, I will go home and shower and come right back," says Alex.

"I will be here; this is what Mr. Stevenson is paying me for," says the nurse.

"If anything happens, call me," says Alex. Alex looked at the nurse and gathered her things. She kissed Leah on the forehead as she stroked her hair back. Alex walked toward the door and turned around. Alex looked back at Leah and the nurse and left. As Alex walked out of the hospital, the sun hit her face. Alex felt the wind on her skin as it whistled by her ear. She soaked it in when she heard "Wow, you're so beautiful." Alex turned to look, and she saw Jamal's sexy face. She smiled so big. Jamal was dressed down in sweatpants, a hoody, and Jordan flip flops. Ladies, I know what you all are thinking—yessss.

Her smile was like Wendy Williams would say, "How you are doing?" It told it all.

"Where are you going, my queen?" says Jamal as he hugs Alex.

"Home to freshen up," says Alex.

"Well, let me drive you, baby. I know you are tired," says Jamal.

"No, I do not want to put you out, sweetheart," says Alex.

"It is no problem, Alex. How is Leah Beloved?" says Jamal.

"Why are you here? Leah is sleeping, and the nurse made me leave" saying Alex? Alex puts her head in her hand.

"I came to check on you and your baby. Also, to update you on some bad news," says Jamal. Alex could only smile inside because she was happy to see him. Alex rarely let anyone see that side of her, but Jamal was her man now. They walked to Jamal's town car and got in.

"What is the bad news?" says Alex.

"The guy came by to do the estimate for the electric chair for the stairs, and it cannot be done," says Jamal.

"Why can it not be done?" says Alex.

"The reason is because you are so fancy, the way the house is set up, your stairs where customized, you would have to knock out the stairs for them to add it," says Jamal.

"Well, knock it out then," says Alex.

"Alex, your house would be under construction for months," says Jamal.

"Leah cannot walk. I have no bedrooms downstairs. I cannot lift her upstairs every day," says Alex.

"I solved your problem, love, but I do not want you to be mad at me," says Jamal.

"Jamal, what did you do?" says Alex. Alex was not sure what he was about to say. She was clinching her pearls.

"I moved you and Leah Beloved in with me. I have plenty of space," says Jamal.

"Wait, you did what?" said Alex. She did not know how to feel.

"Alex, I am sorry," says Jamal.

"Okay, what do you mean you moved us in?" says Alex.

"I turned one of the rooms downstairs into a room for Leah Beloved, and then my homeboy, who owns gyms around the city, is outfitting one of the other rooms downstairs for a physical therapist to come to the house three days a week to help Leah Beloved get back to normal. I have faith in God that she will walk again," says Jamal. Alex just looked at Jamal and started to cry. She was overwhelmed with his generosity. Jamal could see that Alex was happy. Alex had her head down crying when Jamal lifted her head.

"Baby I love you. I just want you happy and stress free," says Jamal. Alex looked into Jamal's eyes and started to kiss him. Alex broke away from the kiss with Jamal.

"I love you too," says Alex. I know what you are thinking. Alex did not just say she loved Jamal because he said it first but she really did love him. He was an amazing man who continued to sweep her off her feet. He always kept her guessing, and he was not predicable at all. Ladies, it is okay to be yourself and let walls down. Jamal and Alex headed to her house so that she could freshen up.

"Do you ever drive yourself?" says Alex.

"Not really, I do not have to," says Jamal. Alex smirked and looked at Jamal.

"Are you hungry, baby?" says Jamal.

"Hell, yes, I am hungry," says Alex. Otis pulled up to Alex's house. Jamal and Alex got out the car and went inside.

"What do you want to eat?" says Jamal.

"Something good that will fill me up," says Alex.

"I have something that will get you full," says Jamal. He stuck his tongue out to Alex. Alex looked at Jamal and laughed.

"You have jokes now," says Alex.

"Not at all, sweetie; I'm just throwing out suggestions," says Jamal.

"I need to go shower and change first," says Alex. Alex and Jamal headed upstairs.

"Yes, sweetie, you do. I was not going to say anything, but yes, you're funky," says Jamal. Alex playfully hit Jamal and walked to her room. When Alex opened the door of her room, there were flowers everywhere.

"Jamal, when did you do this?" says Alex.

"Earlier today," says Jamal.

"You are too sweet. We should go to your aunt's joint," says Alex.

"I'll call her love to see what is on the menu today" says Jamal. Jamal walked in behind her.

"I took the liberty of giving you something to make you feel better; these are for Leah as well" says Jamal.

Alex turned to Jamal, hopped on him, and kissed him. She wrapped her legs around his waist and then fell to the bed. Alex jumped off and headed to take a shower.

"You can come in if you want, sweetie," says Alex. Jamal looked at Alex and followed her to the bathroom.

"I just got out the shower, baby," says Jamal. Alex got to the bathroom and took off all her clothes. Jamal was standing at the door of the bathroom.

"Damn, baby, you are so fine," says Jamal.

"Thank you, I try," says Alex as she smiles. Jamal cannot help but stare at Alex up and down once she got in the shower. Alex peeked around the corner at Jamal, while she was in the shower.

"I could help you, if you need it," says Jamal.

"If you would like to you can," says Alex. Jamal looked at Alex once more and headed to the room. As the water fell off Alex's chocolate body, she massaged the soap on her body to wash off all the hospital smell. Jamal waited for Alex to come out of the shower.

Alex turned off the water and grabbed her towel. Alex walked back in her room to see Jamal laying across her bed. Alex stood in the doorway of the bathroom to watch Jamal for a minute.

"What is wrong, baby," says Jamal?

"Nothing. I'm just admiring you, that is all," says Alex.

"Do you like what you see?" says Jamal.

"I may," says Alex. Alex got her coconut oil off her dresser and started to oil her glistening chocolate body down.

"Damn, the things I could do to you right now," says Jamal as he bites his bottom lip. Jamal wanted Alex so badly, more than before. He had seen Alex at her best and her worst, but he did not care either way. The way she loved her daughter and her passion turned him on. Jamal did not know the feeling he had for her, but he knew he did not want her to leave his side.

"Let me know what you want to do to me," says Alex as she looks at him from the side of her eye.

"You are so sexy to me, I could fuck you all day," says Jamal. Alex looked up and smiled.

"Oh, you could, huh?" says Alex. Alex leaned up to tighten her robe and walked over to the bed where Jamal was laying. Jamal rolled over and looked at Alex from head to toe.

Jamal set up and grabbed on Alex's waist. Every time Jamal touched Alex's, her body melts. It made her get wet instantly. As Alex sat on Jamal's lap, he sucked her ear lobes and sucked on her neck. Jamal sucked on Alex like she was a lollipop. Alex leaned her head back as Jamal's big hands caressed her back. "Baby I'm falling for you" says Jamal. "Why" says Alex? "You complete me, I want to make you the happiest woman alive" says Jamal. Now that statement gave Alex the chills. "Jamal you already make me happy" says Alex. Jamal untied Alex's robe and slid it off her silk dark-skinned body. Her robe slowly fell to the ground by Jamal's feet. Alex lifted Jamal's shirt and hoodie over his head and threw it on the floor. The two started to tongue kiss.

Jamal picked up Alex and laid her on her back. Jamal's arms were ripped, and you could see the veins in his arms. Jamal got on top of Alex, he kissed her neck sucked on her breast. Jamal rubbed on her pearl as he hovered over her. Alex got wet instantly with just the ouch of his finger. Jamal took off his sweats and through them to the side. "I want to make you happy too Jamal" says Alex. Jamal opened Alex's legs wide as he slid his long hard nine inches inside her slowly stroking her. "Alex, I am happy. I can promise you that" says Jamal. "Oh, shit" says Alex. Every time Jamal dove in to Alex. I was like a perfect fit. Alex did her Kegel's so her pussy gripped Jamal's penis every time. "You okay baby" says Jamal as he moaned? "Yesssssss Jamal" says Alex as she moans dragging his name out of her mouth. Alex moaned as she arched her back to make Jamal go deeper. She could feel Jamal, it seemed as if he was touching her soul at this point. Both of their minds were racing with thoughts. Jamal kissed Alex's neck while he continued to please her. Alex moaned and moaned as she grabbed Jamal's arms. Alex called Jamal's name over and over. Alex could not hold back anymore; thick white nut was all over Jamal's penis. "Give it to me baby, nut all over me" says Jamal. Jamal was loving every minute of it. Alex was dealing with a lot and needed this stress release. Jamal was just what the doctor ordered. Jamal made Alex forget everything, it's like when you get that income tax check. You get tunnel vison, can see anyone. "I am about to nut" says Jamal. "I want it all" says Alex. Jamal nutted inside of Alex. He fell to the side of her with sweat dripping down his face. "I needed that Jamal" says Alex. "I needed you" says Jamal.

Alex lifted her head and pinched herself to see if this was a dream. Like she had to be in heaven. But then again God would not be condoning this. "Baby how was Medusa" says Jamal? Alex just moaned. "She was great baby" says Jamal. Now pause for a cause, I know you're wondering who Medusa is. That is what Jamal called Alex's pussy. Why Medusa let me give you a little history on Medusa? I will get back to the scene. Medusa— whose name probably comes from the Ancient Greek word for "guardian." Poets claimed that she had a great boar-like tusk and tongue lolling between her fanged teeth. Writhing snakes were entwining her head in place of hair. Her face was so hideous and her gaze so piercing that the mere sight of her was sufficient to turn a man to stone. I say that to say this the most beautiful thing can be deadly and that's what Alex's pussy was deadly not in a bad way. It took a real man to knock down her walls and let her release herself to him.

Once you had a piece you could not get enough of it. "You know that's my pussy now," says Jamal.

"Yes, I know," says Alex as she laughs. The friction between their bodies was indescribable.

"I love you, Alex Douglas," says Jamal. Alex looked at Jamal as she can see the serenity in his eyes. Alex started to cry but she just smiled. The reason is because she finally had what she had craved for. She had let her guard down for this man.

She looked at him, and she just said it: "I love you too, Jamal," says Alex. Jamal looked into Alex's eyes and kissed her. Alex scooted over to Jamal and laid her head on his chest. Jamal kissed Alex's forehead, and they both fell into a deep sleep. Alex needed this rest; it had been weeks since she was able to get herself together. Nothing could stand between these two now. They were both wide open, and it was no turning back. They both had trusted each other.

It was more than sex; Alex could feel Jamal's soul touch hers. Jamal cared for Alex and her daughter. He wanted nothing but the best for her and Leah Beloved. He knew he could be the man she needed and wanted. He knew that Alex was not weak and loved that about her. Alex knew Jamal was a real man. She needed that love; Coby never gave her what she needed. Alex was attracted to Jamal because he was intelligent and he challenged her. He had his shit together, and he knew how to protect her. That is what she needed.

Chapter 11

The Man Upstairs Always Has the Last Say So

"Anyone can give up, it's the easiest thing in the world to do. But to hold it together is when everyone else would understand if you fell apart, that's true strength."
—*Anonymous*

Yes, Leah was released from the hospital. She had a lot of recovery to do, and Jamal had made life so much easier. Jamal had hired a private nurse to come to the house three days each week to help Leah Beloved with rehab. Alex wanted to get back working, so she could pay off some of these medical bills for Leah Beloved. She was just happy that her baby was home safe at Jamal's house.

Jamal and Alex were in the kitchen getting ready to start cooking.

"Baby, what are you making for us?" says Alex.

"I am making my specialty. Since you want to be nosey and not wait to see, I will be making parmesan-crusted chicken, spinach, sweet potatoes, brown rice, and rolls," says Jamal.

I know what you are thinking, ladies; he is already perfect. What else can he do? This man could not be real, but he was.

"What did I do to deserve this good eating?" says Alex.

"Since you and Leah are staying here, I wanted to show you to what I can do," says Jamal. "Hey baby, has Leah's father called her?"

"No, baby, he has not called and does not need to. I do thank you so much for what you are doing for us," say Alex.

"I do feel think that he should have reached out by now," says Jamal.

"I do not care at this point. I could have lost my child," says Alex.

"Well the investigation is still going on." says Jamal.

"Yes, but I am ready for that to be over with. They found the guys who it did, but they still have questions for Cody," says Alex.

"I know, baby; a coworker of mine is on the case" says Jamal.

"Wait, what, your coworker?" says Alex.

"Yes, and please do not look at me like that. I could not take it because I am too close to this case," says Jamal.

"Jamal, is this person good enough to represent Leah Beloved?" says Alex.

"Yes, baby. You don't think I completely left the case alone do you?" says Jamal.

Jamal knew how important this was to Alex, and that meant it was important to him as well. His coworker knew that. Jamal loved Alex, and nothing was going to mess that up. Alex had a lot on her plate, and he knew that. They were ten and a half months in. He just wanted to take all her problems away and be her knight in shining armor. Little did he know Alex felt the same way. Jamal was a life saver in the midst of all the bullshit. Not to mention, he was always there when she needed him. Jamal had been by Alex's side through Leah's Beloved recovery, which was still a process.

Leah had to learn to walk again, and Alex was taking things hard. Yes, Alex had a man now, but she was still a mother first and foremost. The great thing about it is that Jamal understood that. He helped Leah Beloved on many things. Jamal had also helped Leah get back on track with her school work. He knew how much she loved school, and he admired that. So, while Alex was back and forth between houses and her office. He was there to assist.

Jamal knew Leah Beloved's medical bills were piling up. Alex had not gotten a chance to get to them. Her surgery and recovery in the hospital stay was very high. Alex did not tell Jamal because she felt like he had already done so much, it is not like she didn't have it to pay. This was new for the both of them. They had just gotten together, and she was not going to put her problems on him, even though he didn't mind one bit. When you are a strong, independent woman, you hold things in and together.

Ladies, remember this: never be with a man who will watch you struggle or see things falling down around you. You find a way and take care of things with no help because that is what you are used to. Your business is your business, and that is a fact, but that is not always the right way to go about things. Sometimes being too strong can make you miss out on your blessings. Ladies, if you have a man willing to help, let him. Alex was not used to being vulnerable, but the feeling felt so right. Alex was learning how to bring it down a couple of notches, but it was so hard.

"Sweetheart," says Jamal.

Yes, Jamal," says Alex as she turns around from the sink. She was washing the spinach for the meal.

"I have something to tell you, and I do not want you to be mad. You have to promise me you will not," says Jamal. Jamal was seasoning the chicken to put it on the stove.

"Oh, Lord, what is it?" says Alex as she stares at him. She knew it was going to be something. You never tell a woman not to not to be mad. That makes them mad. You know how many things goes through a woman's mind when she hears that? He does have a child, he is married, he has three baby mommas, he is gay, he really does not like me, or he is broke. Calm down ladies. Let's hear what he has to say.

"Baby I called my homeboy, the doctor. He pulled some strings and told me how much Leah's Beloved bills were. He knows the lady in the billing department," says Jamal.

"Why did you do that, Jamal? You have already done so much," says Alex.

"Hear me out, Alex. I felt like I had to because I really care about you, and I may have overstepped my boundaries, but I had to help out," says Jamal.

"Jamal, what did you do?" says Alex.

"I made a deal," says Jamal as his voice elevated a little. When he did that, it turned Alex on a little. Alex just looked at Jamal in his face; this was finally a man who was putting Alex in her place, and she did not know how to act.

"A deal?" says Alex.

"Alex, the bills are taken care of. The hospital forgave half of the bill because I helped the hospital with a case," says Jamal.

Jamal took a piece of paper out of his pocket and handed it to Alex. Alex grabbed the paper to read it and looked back at Jamal. She dropped her head and started to cry. Alex has money, but she is okay with the fact that he did this for her. This woman has never been spoiled by a man nor treated like the woman she was supposed to be treated. Alex did not know that Jamal was capable of doing this. Jamal brushed his hands off and walked over to Alex to hold her. He gently grabbed her face, lifted her head up, and wiped her tears.

"I'm sorry baby, I overstepped, but lift your head up. I know you still have the bills at your house," says Jamal. Alex was at a loss for words; she didn't know where to start.

"Talk to me sweetie" says Jamal.

"No one has ever done anything for me like this. I cannot tell you how much you mean to me," says Alex.

"Baby, I am here for you. I told you this," says Jamal.

"Why, though? We have not been together long," says Alex. Women tend to question everything.

"Why not? It was no problem," says Jamal. "You are my woman, and I told you being with me is an awesome adventure."

"Baby," says Alex, and she stopped. Jamal reached in to kiss Alex. Jamal gripped Alex's ass and stuck his tongue down Alex's throat. Alex put her arms around Jamal's neck. Jamal lifted Alex up onto the counter. Alex's ass sat firmly on the counter with her cheeks spreading wide. Alex lifted Jamal's shirt up over his head.

"Baby, I have to cook," says Jamal.

"I know, but just a quickie. You have turned me on" says Alex. Jamal laughed and started to suck on Alex's neck. Alex's phone rang.

"Damn, saved by the bell," says Jamal.

"Baby, don't worry about it," says Alex. Jamal continued to kiss Alex on her neck. Alex's phone rang again. Jamal stopped kissing Alex.

"Get the phone, baby," says Jamal. Alex picked up her phone without looking at the caller ID.

"Hello," says Alex with a slight attitude.

"How is my daughter doing?" says Coby. Alex took the phone away from her face, looked at the phone, and looked at Jamal.

Alex mouthed to Jamal that it was Coby. Jamal threw his shirt back on and walked back to the counter to finish seasoning the chicken.

"How can I help you?" says Alex.

"I am checking on my daughter," says Coby.

"It has been weeks since we saw you," says Alex. Jamal looked at Alex and mouthed to Alex to calm down. He was such a peacemaker. Alex could not focus because his lips were so wet and juicy. Seeing him standing in the kitchen turned her on even more.

"Hello," says Coby.

"Yes, Coby, what do you want?" says Alex as she focuses back in.

"Is Leah okay?" saying Coby.

"My baby is fine," saying Alex. Alex hung up the phone in Coby's face and slammed her phone on the counter.

"Alex," says Jamal as he looks at her.

"Yes, Jamal, I do not want to hear it," says Alex.

"Let him know about her; do not block your blessings. You are better than this," says Jamal. Alex rolled her eyes at Jamal and hopped off the counter. Alex knew Jamal was right, but she didn't want to hear it. Jamal was supposed to be on her side. Why should she discuss anything with this low life? Coby was forever causing problems, and Alex was over it. Her phone rang again. Alex picked up her phone; it was Coby again. Alex looked at Jamal before she picked up. Jamal glanced at her and nodded his head at Alex to pick up the phone. Jamal was chopping up the spinach. Alex picked up the phone.

"Hello" says Alex.

"Why did you hang up on me, that shit was rude" says Coby?

"Rude, what's rude is you not being around for your daughter" says Alex. Alex walked out the room as Jamal was still cooking because she didn't want Jamal to see her like this.

"I am not doing this with you today, Coby," says Alex.

"Alex, I didn't mean to get her hurt. It was not my fault," says Coby.

"Now you want to talk, Coby," says Alex.

"I am out of the game now, Alex, I promise. This opened my eyes, I swear," says Coby.

"I cannot or will not trust that. I trusted you, and you let me down again," says Alex. Alex could not trust Coby because he always thought about himself. Alex was hearing Jamal in her head, but at this point it was going in one ear and out the other.

"Alex, Alex," says Coby.

"What, Coby, I am here," says Alex.

"Can I see my baby?" says Coby.

"No, you cannot. Hell no; give her some time," says Alex.

"Why does she need time? I need to explain myself to my child," say Coby.

"She just went through a traumatic experience," says Alex.

"It has been weeks of you not answering me," say Coby.

"I know, and I have been busy; I still work and take care of Leah Beloved," says Alex.

"I understand all that, but I want to see my baby," says Coby as he raised his voice.

"Who the hell do you think you are, making these demands," says Alex.

"Alex, work with me," says Coby.

"Coby, I have to help Leah get dressed. I will call you later," says Alex.

Alex hung the phone up and walked to Leah's new room to check on her. Alex had all types of things going through her head because Coby had lost his mind. Coby had been missing in action. It was a month and some change since Leah had come home from the hospital. She wanted to curse his ass from A to Z, but Jamal had made some valid points. Jamal was lucky he was so fine; that is why Alex listened to him.

Everyone had been calling her, and she had to get back to people. She had not even gotten up with the girls, but they understood. She was getting flowers, cards, and gifts, but really that stuff was for Leah Beloved. Alex did not want to admit it, but she was not as overwhelmed as she was supposed to be. Jamal had really stepped up in more ways than one. She had taken a leave of absence from work, but her boss understood.

Alex walked into Leah's room and saw her reading a book from school. Leah's room was so pretty; she loved unicorns and sparkles anything. Leah Beloved's theory was that a unicorn is hard to come by, and when you find one, it is rare. Alex always taught Leah to never show your full abilities to your opponent or let anyone in your game room.

"Hey, baby, what are you doing?" says Alex.

"I'm catching up on homework, Mom, but it is hard," saying Leah Beloved.

"Leah, you need to relax. You have time to catch up, sweetheart," says Alex.

"Mom, I do not," says Leah, talking with frustration.

"Leah, you were shot, baby. You need to chill," says Alex.

"Mom, I am going back to school. I cannot let this get me down," says Leah.

"No, you are not going to school. I am hiring a tutor for you in the meantime," says Alex.

As Alex had this conversation with Leah, she thought she was talking to a grown woman. Yes, Alex was a little hard on Leah, but Leah was too hard on herself. Alex wanted her to know that it is okay to give yourself a break. She did not want Leah to overwhelm herself.

"Mom, why are you looking like that?" say Leah.

"You are an amazing child," says Alex.

"How will you know if it is too much if you do not let me try first?" says Leah. Leah had Alex thinking hard. Alex had to clinch her pearls, she couldn't believe Leah was saying this. After all, this is what she taught her.

"Leah, we will talk about it later. Are you ready to eat?" says Alex.

"No, Mom, I am not hungry," says Leah.

"Why not?" says Alex.

"Mom, I just am not because of the medicine has me feeling weird," says Leah.

"Okay, baby, let me know when you are. Do you want some yogurt or apple sauce?" says Alex.

Okay, Mom, I will let you know, I invited Bria over. Mom, is that okay?" says Leah.

"Yes, sweetie, that is fine," says Alex. Alex's phone rang, and the doorbell rang also.

"Jamal, you want me to get the door?" says Alex.

"No, baby, Marta has it," says Jamal. Alex walked back to the kitchen.

"I have a surprise for you," says Jamal. As soon as Jamal said it, Michelle walked around the corner.

"Hey, boo," says Michelle. Alex looked so shocked; she hugged Michelle so hard.

"Hey, girl," says Alex. Bria stood there looking crazy.

"Where is Leah, Auntie Alex?" says Bria.

"She is in that first room to the right," says Alex.

"Jamal, thanks for inviting me," says Michelle.

"No problem," says Jamal.

"Thank you," says Alex. She goes around the counter to kiss Jamal.

"This house is nice," says Michelle. Alex walked out the kitchen to make sure Bria got to Leah Beloved's room. Alex opened the door.

"Are y'all okay?" says Alex.

Both girls chanted together, "We are good." Alex laughed and went back into the kitchen. The doorbell rings again.

"Marta, can you get that, please," says Jamal as he yells towards the kitchen door.

"Yes sir," says Marta.

"Wait, what smells so good?" says Michelle.

"Girl, Jamal is cooking for us," says Alex.

"Damn, he cooks too," said Michelle.

"Yes, he does, among other things," says Alex. Michelle leans over the counter to whisper to Alex.

"I know the sex is good because you don't let anyone around your child or in your space," says Michelle.

"Girl, you know me so well," saying Alex as she smiles. Honestie comes around the corner with a bottle of wine.

"Hey, ladies and Jamal," says Honestie.

"What are you doing here?" says Alex.

"Well, damn, that's rude," says Honestie.

"You know I did not mean it like that," says Alex. She heads toward Honestie to give her a hug. Honestie placed the wine on the counter.

"I was invited by the man of the house," says Honestie.

"Jamal, you continue to surprise me," says Alex. Jamal looks up from cooking the chicken and smiles.

"I know you needed girl time, love, so I invited all the girls over," says Jamal.

"You have a good one," says Honestie. Jamal laughs at Honestie.

"Marta," says Jamal. Marta comes around the corner.

"Can you set up the theater for the little ladies?" says Jamal.

"Yes sir," says Marta.

"Thank you, Marta," says Jamal. Marta walks out of the kitchen.

"There is a theater in here?" says Alex.

"Yes, love, down that hallway," says Jamal.

"You did know that?" says Honestie.

"This is not my house. I do not snoop," says Alex as she looks at Honestie.

"Correction, this is your house as well," says Jamal as he gave Alex the side eye. Alex clinched her pearls.

"You heard him," says Michelle.

"Do you all want some wine ladies?" says Alex.

"Of course, we do," says Michelle and Honestie in unison. Alex reaches in the overhead cabinet and grabs three wine glasses.

"Baby, do you want some wine?" says Alex. Alex grabbed another glass from the cabinet. Alex placed her phone on the counter.

"Just a little," says Jamal. She starts to pour the wine into their glasses.

"Hey, Jamal, what are you making?" says Michelle.

"You will see if I can get done," says Jamal as he looks at Alex.

"Why are you looking at me?" says Alex.

"You know why," says Jamal as he smiles. The girls did not know that they were about to get things popping before Alex's phone rung.

"Jamal, we will be in the garden to talk about girl things," says Alex.

"You cannot go out there—go in the den if you do not mind," says Jamal.

"Yes sir," says Alex.

"I will call you ladies when dinner is ready," says Jamal.

"Thank you. I love you!" says Alex, and she smiles at him.

"I love you more," says Jamal. The girls head to the den to sit on the round couches.

"Where is Camilla?" says Alex.

"Late as always," says Michelle. Alex sits down, and so does Michelle and Honestie.

"So, what's the tea? Seems like we have not talked in a minute," says Michelle.

"I am not sure where to start, but girl, Jamal has been there every step of the way. I can't thank him enough," says Alex.

"A blind man can see that," says Honestie.

"Has Coby called?" says Michelle.

"Coby continues to call, and Jamal made me talk to him today," says Alex.

"Made you talk to him?" say Michelle with a confused face,

"Yes, his fine ass made me talk to him. I can't tell him no, girl," says Alex as she smiles.

"Talk about what, because quite frankly, y'all have nothing to discuss in my eyes," says Michelle.

'He wants to see Leah Beloved and explain himself and all this other bullshit," says Alex.

"I'm dead like *The First 48* red tape, girl. Please stop it," says Michelle.

"Jamal says I should not block my blessings and just communicate with Coby," says Alex. Before Alex could say anything, Jamal came into the den.

"Excuse me ladies, baby, your phone is ringing. It's Camilla. I wouldn't have looked at it, but she called like three times," says Jamal.

"Thank you, baby," says Alex. Jamal handed Alex her phone and walked back to the kitchen on the other side of the house. Alex answers the phone.

"Hello, chick, where are you?" says Alex.

"I am at the door," says Camilla.

"It's about time. Just ring the doorbell; we are in the den waiting on you," says Alex. Alex hangs up her phone.

"So, are you going to tell us how you started living here?" says Michelle. Honestie sips her wine.

"Yes, because Miss "I don't need a man for shit" is living life, honey," says Honestie. Alex smiles hard. Alex is about to tell the girls the tea when Camilla walks around the corner.

"The party is here," says Camilla.

"Girl, sit your late ass down," says Honestie.

"Do not hate. Alex, this house is laid," says Camilla.

"I told y'all, but Jamal has been amazing. He just set this whole thing up, he moved us in and is making Leah Beloved feel so comfortable," says Alex.

"See that is what I need in my life," says Camilla.

"This makes me miss my man," says Michelle.

"He even got the hospital to forgive half of her bill," says Alex. The girls laughed and caught up. The night was nothing but amazing. This is what Alex needed. Yes, she has a man now, but you always need that girl time.

"A wise girl knows her limits, a smart girl knows she has none."
—Marilyn Monroe

Chapter 12

Let's Sip This Tea

"I am not afraid of storms for I am still learning how to sail my ship."
—Louisa May Alcott

Alex's phone rang. "Hey, love, what's up?" says Alex.

"Nothing. Are your busy tonight?" says Michelle.

"No, hun. I am just going to catch up on paperwork now that I can get back to these coins," says Alex.

"I know you're not at the office," says Michelle. Alex was easing her way back into work because she knew that she had to stack her bank back up. Though it was still sitting pretty, she never wanted it to go under a certain amount. Alex always hustled like she was broke. That is what a real boss does, never stopping to think about what they can spend money on. It's all in what more you can invest in. Grow your business and yourself at the same time.

"No, I am at the house since you have my child," says Alex.

"I want to have a dinner at my house for just the girls," says Michelle.

"Okay, you know I am down for the food anytime," says Alex.

"I am going to have it catered, and we all need to get together," says Michelle.

"Well, let me know a time, and I will be there," saying Alex.

Michelle was right; they did need a girl's night, just for getting back to the basis with things. It had been a couple of weeks since they got together.

"Okay, hun, let me call the other girls to see if they can fix me in their schedules. I am leaning towards eight p.m.," says Michelle.

"Okay, boo, I will be there," says Alex.

Alex was now getting into the swing of things and getting her life back on track. With Leah back and forth in physical therapy and going back to school, Alex was getting her work life back, her love life with Jamal, and her friends. She had a lot on her plate. Coby was still calling, asking for Leah. *Why should I let him talk to her? Is Leah ready to talk to her father?* Alex thought to herself. She knew that she was not going to let him be in her life right now because losing her baby was not an option. Coby was not going to pop in and pop out when he wanted to.

Sitting home in the bed, going through paperwork, she got sleepy and dosed off. Alex had been sleeping for three hours when she popped up out her sleep. She had six missed calls and two voicemails. Two of the missed calls were from Jamal, one from Leah Beloved, one from Michelle, and Camilla called. Alex sat up and got her head together. She looked back at her phone and went to call everyone back.

Alex called Leah, saying, "Hey, baby, are you okay?"

"Yes, Mommy, I am," says Leah.

"Why did you call me, baby girl?" says Alex.

"I wanted to know if I can spend the night at Aunt Michelle's," says Leah.

"Do you think that's a good idea?" says Alex.

"Mom, I will be fine," says Leah.

"Okay, well, I will be over there in an hour and a half to bring your stuff," says Alex.

"Thank you so much. Mommy. I love you," says Leah.

"I love you more," says Alex. Alex hung up with Leah and called Michelle.

"Hey, boo, what's up?" says Alex.

"Girl, what were you doing?" says Michelle.

"I was asleep," says Alex.

"Finally, you got some rest. How does that feel?" says Michelle.

"It was great. I feel so good," says Alex.

"Girl, my man called me today; he says he has good news," says Michelle.

"Okay, hun, I'll be ready to hear it," says Alex.

"I was calling because Leah wants to spend the night," says Michelle.

"That's fine, I will be there later anyway. I'll bring her medicine and her clothes with me as well," says Alex.

"Okay, hun, I will see you tonight at 8 p.m. sharp," says Michelle.

"Okay, Michelle, I will be there. Let me go because my man is calling me. Let me see if he wants this chocolate before I pull up on you, boo," says Alex.

"Oh, Lord, bye girl," says Michelle. Alex was smiling from ear to ear when she called Jamal.

"Hey, my sexy black queen, how are you?" says Jamal.

"I am rested. I was sleeping, baby," says Alex.

"Finally, I have been trying to get you to rest for days," says Jamal.

"Why is everyone saying that?" says Alex.

"Alex you have not been sleep since Leah Beloved came home," says Jamal.

"How can I sleep when I must keep an eye on my baby?" says Alex.

"Babe, Stella asked to come back to work to help. You need to take advantage of that. I do not have kids yet, but I understand that you cannot be your best for her if you are not your best," says Jamal. Jamal always knew the right thing to say. He was so wise.

"I know, and I think I am going to let her; I need to get back to work," says Alex.

"I can dig that, baby," says Jamal.

"How are you doing, love," says Alex?

"Babe, I am good. I just miss you and was checking on you. I am on the way to the house now," says Jamal.

"Well, you miss me," says Alex as she laughs a bit?

"Yes, I do, hunny," says Jamal.

"What do you miss about me?" says Alex. Alex felt like she was a kid again. You know, when you used to have a crush and you all stay up all night on the phone and pass notes back and forth in class? Yes, Alex was in love with Jamal. She thought it was a dream, and she did not want to wake up from it. *Someone pinch me,* she said in her head.

"I miss your smart-ass mouth," says Jamal as he laughs.

"So, you have jokes?" says Alex.

"Yes, I do. love, but on a serious note. are you busy tonight?" says Jamal.

"Yes, I am. Michelle invited all us girls to her house for dinner so that we can catch up. Leah Beloved is already there," says Alex.

"Babe, I have something to tell you that is important," says Jamal.

"What do you have to tell me?" says Alex.

"I would rather tell you in person. I am outside; I'll be up there in a minute," says Jamal.

"I am in the room," says Alex.

"I cannot get enough of you, Alex," says Jamal.

"Same here, love," says Alex. Alex and Jamal hung up the phone.

Alex hopped out of bed. She ran in her bathroom and brushed her teeth. Alex took off her relaxed clothes and waited on Jamal to come in the house. She had on a piece of lingerie from a company that she thought about investing in. Alex was posing in the mirror when she heard an argument outside. She threw on her robe and headed downstairs. Alex opened the front door to see Coby's ass standing in the driveway to her surprise.

"Why are you at our house?" says Jamal. Alex walked out the door.

"I want to see my daughter," says Coby. Alex stepped from behind Jamal.

"How the fuck did you find us?" says Alex.

"I want to see my daughter. and you will not let me or answer the phone." says Coby.

"I have nothing to say to you, and now you can get off my property because you are trespassing," says Alex. Coby looked at Alex and Jamal.

"Alex, I need to see her," says Coby.

"She is not here, and you are causing a scene," says Alex.

"So now she's not here. Bitch, you lie," says Coby.

"Before Alex could say what she wanted to, Jamal stopped her.

"Get in the house, Alex," says Jamal.

"Jamal, he will not call out my name," says Alex.

"I said, get in the house," says Jamal. Sometimes you have to let your man be the man. He will do things and move certain ways because of who he is, if he has good sense. Alex turned around to walk in the house, but she could see Coby still standing there.

"Alex you heard me" says Coby. It took everything for Alex not to tear his ass a new asshole.

"You can leave now, bro," says Jamal. Jamal walked in behind her and shut the door, then locked it. Jamal was not afraid of him, but Jamal knew the right way to handle this situation. He had shit to lose, and he was not with Coby's shit.

Coby knocked on the door. Alex and Jamal stood in the foyer.

"I know you want to curse his ignorant ass out, but you and I both have shit to lose," says Jamal.

"You are right, baby, but you saved his ass," says Alex.

"I am going to call the police," says Jamal.

"Call them. I need to get dressed" says Alex. Coby had crossed the damn line when he came to their home. That was her domain, her place of rest. Alex looked at Jamal, his fine ass was turning her on because he was serious, and she had never seen him this way. Jamal called the police. He and Alex headed upstairs.

"I am not scared of the cops," yells Coby. They could hear Coby still at the door.

Jamal looked at Alex. Alex was getting dressed for the dinner. She grabbed her phone to text Michelle to tell her that she was going to be late.

"I am so sorry for this; I do not know how he found out where we live," says Alex.

"Why are you apologizing to me?" says Jamal.

"He is the father of my child," says Alex.

"The police will be here in thirty minutes. Alex, I know you do not deal with him, so it's fine, love" says Jamal. Jamal was a real man. He loved Alex, and she knew that.

"You turn me on even more," says Alex.

"I am glad I showed up when I did," says Jamal.

"I am too, because I would have shot his ass," says Alex.

"Baby, you cannot do that; you have too much to lose," says Jamal. Jamal always knew what to say in certain situations when hell was going on.

"You have Michelle's thing, right?" says Jamal.

"Yes, I do. baby. I want to thank you for everything that you do for me and Leah Beloved." says Alex. Jamal walked over to Alex. Alex looked up and smiled at Jamal. He kissed her and sat on the bed to watch her get dressed.

"You do not have to even have to thank me. I love you and Leah Beloved." says Jamal. Alex was surprised at what Jamal had said.

"Damn. you will not make me cry off my lashes." says Alex. Jamal laughed so hard. Jamal looked in the direction that Alex was in and thought to himself about how lucky a man he was. Alex was an amazing woman.

"Sweetheart. come here." says Jamal.

"Baby. I need to get dressed." says Alex.

"I know but you have something on your back." says Jamal.

"What is it?" says Alex as she tried to look at her back in the mirror.

"Come here, and I will get it off," says Jamal.

Alex walked over to Jamal, and he placed his hand on her back.

"What was is it, baby?" says Alex. She knew she was going to have to change.

"My hand," says Jamal as he caressed her body. Jamal knew just how to touch Alex. With every touch, Jamal knew it would make Alex wet. Alex's body always had a tingling feeling going down her spine whenever Jamal touched her. Jamal knew that he could get Alex to make love to him whenever he wanted her to. He had this sexy vibe about him. That shit turned Alex on so much, when she looked at him, she couldn't help but picture them having sex.

"Jamal stop playing, I told you I have to get dressed to go," says Alex.

"You can go wherever you need to go—once you give me what's between those legs," said Jamal.

"You trying to keep me hostage," says Alex. Alex looked at him and could not resist; look at him. He was looking at Alex like he wanted to eat her. She was going to let him do just that. Jamal and Alex were smiling at each other. Jamal got off the bed and picked Alex up.

"Put me down," says Alex.

"Make me," says Jamal in his bedroom voice. Jamal started to kiss Alex's neck when her phone rung.

"Do not pick it up," says Jamal.

"I have to; it could be Leah Beloved," says Alex. Jamal put Alex down so she could grab her phone.

"Hello," says Alex.

"Where are you?" saying Michelle?

"I am home. I had a situation. I am coming," says Alex.

"It is a 911 emergency, and you need to get to my house now," says Michelle.

"Okay, Michelle, calm down. I'm finishing putting on my clothes, and I will be there. Is my child okay?" saying Alex?

"Okay, I hear you. She is fine," says Michelle. Michelle hung up the phone, and Alex looked at Jamal.

"Do not be mad. I have to go, and you do not know how to do quickies," says Alex.

"I'm not being rushed to please you," says Jamal. Alex rolled her eyes and put on her shoes. Alex kissed Jamal and ran downstairs to leave.

"Wait, baby," says Jamal.

"Yes, Jamal," says Alex.

"I am going to walk you out. I do not trust him," says Jamal. Alex and Jamal walked outside. Coby was sitting in his car. The police pulled up. Alex got into her car as the officer walked up the driveway.

"Just wait up for me, baby," says Alex.

"I'm not going anywhere," says Jamal. Jamal tongue kissed Alex. Alex hopped in her car to head to Michelle's house. As Alex pulled out the driveway, she and Coby locked eyes. Alex looked back up the driveway. The officer and Jamal were heading toward Coby's car. Driving off, Alex started to play "Remy Ma Conceited" in her car. Alex was already feeling herself because she was fine as fuck, of course, but she had a man finally. A good man, a man who wanted just her and to please her.

Let me tell you when you have a man who caters to you and makes sure you are good. Hold on to him; there are still good men out there in the world. Trust me when I tell you, and they are ready to suck and lick every part of your body and to pay some bills if you let them. I am not saying that is all you want, but the end goal is bliss, to live happy with one person and to just live life in this cold world. Alex was rapping the words, yes, she still had a little hood in her, don't judge her. That was the song of the century. Alex pulled up to Michelle's house and got out of the car. Alex walked through the door dancing.

"Hey, chick, the boss is here," says Alex.

"Hey boo, you can have a seat at the table," says Michelle.

"Where is Honestie and Camilla?" says Alex. Before Michelle could speak, Honestie walked in.

"The queen is here," saying Honestie.

"Oh Lord, girl, sit down. Y'all happy as hell," says Michelle.

"Yes, ma'am," says Honestie as she laughed at Michelle.

"Let me see where Camilla is," says Alex.

"Yes, call her late ass," says Michelle. Alex picked up her phone and pressed Camilla's name to call it. Camilla walked through the door.

"I am here, damn, I know one of you heifers was about to call me," says Camilla.

"Someone is a little grumpy," says Honestie.

"Shut up," says Camilla.

"Everyone sit down, please," says Michelle. The ladies took their seats and waited on further instructions.

"So why did we have to get in our Sunday best to come over here for this lavash dinner?" says Honestie.

"I will tell you ladies in just a minute," says Michelle.

"What is the 911?" says Alex.

Michelle sits at the table. "We can now eat," says Michelle. The chef came over and started placing the lady's plates in front of them. On the menu was Brown Sugar Lemon Garlic Butter Salmon, loaded potatoes, asparagus, and creamy mac and cheese. As soon as Camilla's food was placed in front of her, she ran to the bathroom and threw up.

"Okay, Godfather," says Alex.

"What the hell is wrong with her?" says Honestie. Honestie was that friend who peeped everything. She knew the tea before you told her. It was a gift of hers.

"I do not know," says Alex as she looked puzzled. The ladies started to eat, and they waited for Camilla to come back to the table.

"This food is delicious," says Alex.

"You can thank Chef Pierre for the amazing food," says Michelle. Camilla came back to the table.

"You okay, hun," says Alex?

"Yea I'm good," says Camilla. Camilla was lying through her teeth.

"Okay, say something," says Honestie.

"Okay, so what is this big news that you have for us? I am not feeling well, love," says Camilla.

"Damn, you all are so impatient," says Michelle.

"You know this already," says Alex. Michelle gets up with her glass in her hand.

"I just closed a deal with International Cosmetics Group, and my product will be sold in stores all over the world now," says Michelle as she screams. The girls got up and screamed with her. This is what you call support, ladies; support your friends whether they are doing better than you or not. Real friends are happy for you no matter what. Y'all can all win together. When one comes up, all come up.

"Okay that is not all. I just got an advance for one million, so I am taking all of us on an all-expense paid trip to Dubai," says Michelle.

"Wait what?" says Honestie.

"I'm ready, so when do we leave?" says Alex. Alex is down for anything; she never cared whether it was breaking and entering, a stakeout, or even keying your cheating man's car. Alex was that friend; she rarely had questions.

"I have to check my schedule," says Camilla.

"You always have to check your schedule," says Michelle.

"I cannot or will not go back and forth with you right now," says Camilla as she got up to go to the bathroom again. Michelle looks at Honestie.

"What is her problem?" says Alex.

"I am going. I am packing my bags tonight when I get home," says Honestie.

"I am so proud of you, boo; you did it," says Alex.

"Thank you, hun, that is not all. I told the company that they had no deal unless I went through you company, Honestie" says Michelle.

Honestie's eyes started to water.

"What the fuck, are you serious?" says Honestie.

"I am so serious; this is not a game," says Michelle.

"This is only the beginning," says Alex. As the girls finished up their food and laughed and talked. Camilla came out the bathroom, looking confused.

"What did I miss?" says Camilla. Camilla could not enjoy herself. She needed to tell the girls what was on her mind and her secret. But, how could she? She did not want the judgment from anyone. The girls moved from the table to the living room area.

"This is so crazy. I was just telling Paul I wanted to expand," says Honestie.

"Ladies, I cannot stay long. I have my man waiting patiently for me. Michelle, is Leah okay to stay the night?" says Alex.

"Why wouldn't she be?" says Michelle.

"Oh, your man, so you get a man and cannot hang with us girls anymore?" says Camilla.

"Girl, you are snapping on everyone tonight," says Honestie.

"What?" says Alex. "I know. right. and that's not the case. I have been here for four hours."

"Girl, you're good. I wish my husband was home because y'all would not be here," says Michelle as she laughed with her head back. Michelle's house phone rang.

"Let me get up to get that; it is late as hell. It has to be one of my VIP customers," says Michelle.

"Your what?" says Alex. Alex ignored Camilla's comment because she had to be going through something, and Alex was going to get to the bottom of the bullshit.

"My VIP customers, some of them have my house number if the need outside normal work hour services," says Michelle.

Oh, okay, I didn't know that was an option," says Honestie.

"Yes, it is when you are paying $1000.00 for your hair."

"Oh, excuse me, everybody is not able," says Honestie.

"Girl, stop with the lies; you make over a million dollars a year," says Alex.

"Hello," says Michelle.

"Hello, baby, how are you?" says Michelle's husband.

"Hello, baby, it is late, and how are you calling me?" says Michelle. All the girls turned around to see what Michelle was talking about.

"Baby, they are letting me out tomorrow. I am at a private facility," says Michelle's husband.

"What are you serious?" screams Michelle.

"What is going on?" says Alex.

Michelle puts up a finger for the girls to be quiet.

"Yes, baby, I am a free man tomorrow," says Michelle's husband.

"Where do I need to go to pick you up?" says Michelle.

"I will give you more details in the morning." says Michelle's husband.

"Why can't you tell me now?" says Michelle.

"Baby, trust me, I will call you in the morning. I love you," says Michelle's husband.

"I love you more, baby," says Michelle. They hung up the phone. Michelle was so shocked that she forgot to tell her husband the good news.

"Okay, so are you going to tell us what happened?" says Camilla. Michelle just stood in silence. She could not speak; she just cried and cried. The girls sat in silence with her for a minute. Michelle walked over to where the girls were and sat down.

"So, my husband is coming home tomorrow," says Michelle. Everyone got up and screamed and jumped up and down.

"Wait how? I thought he had five more years to go," says Honestie.

"He did, but he was told he will tell me all the details in the morning," says Michelle.

"Look at God," says Alex.

"That's crazy," says Camilla as she rushed to the bathroom once again.

"I have no details as of yet; he had to go," says Michelle.

"Wow, I know you are happy," says Alex. Michelle and her husband had a love that no one could touch. They had been together for twenty years and counting. Michelle saw no other man. She loved Marcus, and Marcus loved her. They say the childish love never lasts, but Michelle and Marcus proved everyone wrong. Neither one of them cheated or thought about calling it quits. Yes, they had some rough times, but they always worked through it. Marcus loved Michelle for her loyalty, and it could not be matched. They had that basketball love, that Gabriel union, and Dwayne Wade love, and that fat kid who loves cake for breakfast love. Alex knew Jamal may be the man for her, but she also did not want to get her heart broken again. "Well, pour another drink," says Honestie.

"Yes, pour me one as well," says Alex.

"I cannot drink, and I need it," says Camilla.

Alex sat and started to reflect on these last couple of months she had spent with Jamal. She looked at Michelle to see how happy she was that her husband was getting out and being able to come home, and she wanted that same joy. Alex knew what Jamal could be for her.

"Ladies, I have to call it a night; my man is waiting for me," says Alex.

"I need to go as well; I do not feel well," says Camilla. Alex and Camilla got up to head to the door. They both turned around to give Michelle and Honestie hugs.

"Y'all be safe, and let me know when you all get home," says Michelle.

"Will do," says Alex. They both walked out the door.

"Camilla text me when you get home," says Alex as she got into her car.

"I will," says Camilla. Alex turned on her radio and texted Jamal to tell him she was coming home. Alex backed out the driveway to head home. She turned on "Ella Mai-Naked" and started to sing along. Alex drove to Jamal's house to see her man. As Alex pulled into the driveway, there were balloons all the way up the driveway. Alex parked her car and stepped out of the car, and there were rose petals at her feet. Alex walked up to her door, and it was cracked. Her first thought was: *This is how all black people die first.* Jamal was a solider, so she sucked it up. Alex walked through the door to see a trail of rose petals down her hallway. She walked in to hear music playing with the song "Matrimony" by Wale, featuring Usher. Alex was led into the garden by the rose pedals. When she got to the door that led to the garden, Alex saw Jamal standing in the middle of candles that were shaped in a heart. Roses and candles were everywhere. He had on a black Armani suit with black shoes. He looked so good that Alex wanted to jump on him.

"What is going on, Jamal," says Alex. Next to Jamal was a projector. Jamal turned it on, and on the screen were Leah Beloved, Michelle, Bria, and Honestie on one screen. The next screen had her mom on Skype, and the last screen showed Alex's sisters. Alex was not expecting this from Jamal.

"Baby, come in; do not be scared," says Jamal.

"Jamal, what is this?" says Alex.

"Baby just enjoy the moment. Come stand right here," says Jamal as he turned down the music. Alex walked to the spot where Jamal had pointed to. Jamal started to speak to Alex.

"I have loved you from the first time that I saw you in that club. We have shared so much together in this short period of time, but you have showed me the woman that you are. I know that I do not want to be without you because you make me so much better. I love you and Leah Beloved, and nothing can change that. Jamal got down on one knee in front of Alex. "Alexandria Douglas, will you marry me and make me the happiest man alive?" says Jamal.

Jamal held this ten-karat ring in front of Alex. Alex was shaking and crying; she did not know what to say. Alex did not know why this was happening to her. With all the bad luck in her life, she was finally getting something good.

"Girl, you had better answer him, or I will," says Alex's mom. Everyone laughed. Ladies, I know what you are saying in your head. It's like a horror movie when you are screaming at the TV, telling the person to run. Alex wanted to scream, *hell yes.*

"Baby, are you okay?" says Jamal. Alex was speechless; she could not let the words come out or move for that matter. Her mind was playing tricks on her, and she knew it. So many thoughts were going through her head that she just could not think straight.

"Baby, what is wrong? Talk to me," says Jamal. Mind you, he is still on one knee. Alex finally spoke.

"I am scared; what if we do not work? What if you cheat on me? What if your family does not like me?" says Alex. Yes, she was throwing all these questions at Jamal. No matter what you have in your head, God's got you. He will never leave your side. When you have been through so much bullshit time after time, just know that there is light at the end of the tunnel. It is your turn, boo; just go for it.

"Baby, I've got you, I will treat you like the queen you are and give you the things you deserve. You are my beautiful black queen. I will cherish the ground you walk on as I do now," says Jamal. Alex looked at Jamal, and her lips just moved.

"Yes, I will marry you, baby," says Alex. Everyone screamed.

Alex knew in her mind that she could not get anything better than what was in front of her. This man loved her, and he did not want anything from her but her heart. Here is the thing, when someone truly loves you, they will show you. They will stick it out with you and show you that they are for you. Do not be scared to go the distance with someone because that person can make you the happiest that you have ever been. Jamal got off his knee and kissed Alex.

"I love you, baby," says Jamal.

"I love you too, Jamal," says Alex. Jamal kissed Alex once more and headed toward the screen.

"Leah Beloved, I want to thank you for helping me plan this and giving me your blessing," says Jamal.

"No problem," says Leah Beloved. Jamal reached in his pocket and took out another box. There was another ring in the box. Alex looked at Jamal; she was not sure what was going on. Jamal got on one knee in front of the screen.

"Leah Beloved Douglas, I am not only marrying your mom, I am marrying you as well," says Jamal. Alex walked over to the screen, she could see Leah shedding a tear. Alex stood next to Jamal.

"Leah, I have watched you be so brave the past couple months, and you have showed me that you are a fighter. I want you to be my daughter on your terms. I am not trying to replace your father by any means. Can I be your number two dad?" says Jamal. Alex looked at Jamal and started to cry. and she looked at the Leah Beloved for her answer.

"Yes, sir. I accept." says Leah Beloved with tears in her eyes. Every was crying and emotional. Jamal had done it again. Could this man be more perfect? If a person elevates you, cherishes you, makes you become better, and challenges you, keep that person by your side. I know life can be hard, but you need someone who will be your peace; someone that you can talk to and share your thoughts with is always a plus. You have to learn how to give and take. Relationships are like a job. You have to continue to work hard and put the work in.

Through all the mess, Alex realized Camilla was not in the mix.

"Where is Camilla?" says Alex.

"I do not know, but let me see that ring, boo," says Honestie. Alex put her ring up to the screen to show everyone.

"Baby, your phone is ringing," says Jamal.

"Answer it, baby," says Alex.

"Hello," says Jamal. Jamal could hear crying in the background.

"Jamal?" says Camilla.

"Yes, what is wrong?" says Jamal.

"I hope I did not mess up the surprise, but I really need to speak to Alex," says Camilla as she is crying.

"Okay, stop crying; you did not interrupt anything we just got finished," says Jamal. Jamal walked over to Alex with her phone. He mouthed to Alex: "She is crying." Alex was looking at her phone confused, she grabbed her phone from Jamal. Alex kissed Jamal one more time.

"Hello," says Alex.

"I know you are busy, but I need to tell you something," says Camilla.

"Why are you crying?" says Alex.

"I have something to tell you," says Camilla.

"What is it?" says Alex. Alex looked at the phone and was lost for words.

Ladies remember that you can have it all: the career, the life, taking care of your kids, dating, and being happy. Do not settle for less. You deserve so much that you can tap into. Strive for greatness. Say what you want out of life. Put your foot down, and set goals for yourself. Stand on your principles. There will be roadblocks because nothing in life is easy. All you have to do is push and continue to be great. Nothing worth fighting for is easy.

"I will love you as long as the sun burns in the sky, as long as the moon shines its life into the dark night, until the raging blue oceans become calm and run dry. I will love you until the end of time"
—Christy Ann Martine

CPSIA information can be obtained
at www.ICGtesting.com
Printed in the USA
LVHW110953220820
663895LV00003B/674

9 781632 210173